The discovery of the
unleashes a weapon of

One touch from the Spear of Odin can transform a man into a *berserker*—an unstoppable rage-fueled killing machine. Dane Maddock and "Bones" Bonebrake, former Navy SEALs turned treasure hunters, are on assignment in Norway—their mission: Stop the rogue biotech company ScanoGen from getting their hands on the legendary weapon.

But ScanoGen isn't the only enemy they'll need to worry about. A crazed mercenary with delusions of godhood has plans to use the spear to raise an army of *berserkers*, unleashing them upon an unsuspecting world, and only Dane and Bones stand in his way.

Praise for the Dane Maddock Adventures

A great read that provides lots of action, and thoughtful insight as well, into strange realms that are sometimes best left unexplored." *Paul Kemprecos, author of Cool Blue Tomb*

"A non-stop thrill ride triple threat- smart, funny and mysterious!" Jeremy Robinson, author of Instinct and Threshold

"David Wood has done it again. Quest takes you on an expedition that leads down a trail of adventure and thrills!" David L. Golemon, Author of the Event Group series

BERSERK

A DANE MADDOCK ADVENTURE

DAVID WOOD
MATT JAMES

Berserk
Copyright 2017, 2018 by David Wood

Published by Adrenaline Press
www.adrenaline.press

Adrenaline Press is an imprint of Gryphonwood Press
www.gryphonwoodpress.com

Edited by Sean Ellis

This is a work of fiction. All characters are products of
the authors' imaginations or are used fictitiously.

ISBN-13: 978-1-940095-87-5
ISBN-10: 1-940095-87-5

BOOKS and SERIES by DAVID WOOD

The Dane Maddock Adventures
Dourado
Cibola
Quest
Icefall
Buccaneer
Atlantis
Ark
Xibalba
Loch
Solomon Key

Dane and Bones Origins
Freedom
Hell Ship
Splashdown
Dead Ice
Liberty
Electra
Amber
Justice
Treasure of the Dead

Adventures from the Dane Maddock Universe
Destination-Rio
Destination-Luxor
Berserk
The Tomb
Devil's Face
Outpost

Arcanum
Magus
Brainwash
Herald
Maug

Jade Ihara Adventures (with Sean Ellis)
Oracle
Changeling
Exile

Bones Bonebrake Adventures
Primitive
The Book of Bones
Skin and Bones
Venom

Jake Crowley Adventures (with Alan Baxter)
Blood Codex
Anubis Key

Brock Stone Adventures
Arena of Souls
Track of the Beast (forthcoming)

Myrmidon Files (with Sean Ellis)
Destiny
Mystic

Sam Aston Investigations (with Alan Baxter)
Primordial
Overlord

PROLOGUE

"**What's your hurry**, brother?" Sigurd asked, shivering against the cold. It was unusually bitter for the time of year and a harbinger of the season to come. While both men were used to the dipping temperatures, neither preferred them.

Johan glanced back, wondering how much to tell his twin.

Growing up, they had always known what each other was thinking. The two men were exact duplicates of one another in every way. Not only were they identical twins, but they had always acted and dressed the same. But life had taken them in very different directions.

Sigurd Larsen was one of the wealthiest men in the region, largely due to his lucrative timber business. He was also deeply devoted to God.

Johan, a man of the land, had very different priorities. He begrudgingly worked part-time for his brother if only to make their mother worry less.

They had often gone on long hikes in their younger years, spending days, even weeks, in the woods, but as time passed and Sigurd became more involved in running his business, they spent less time together, and the differences between them magnified.

Johan knew he couldn't keep this secret from his brother forever. He halted and breathed in deeply. As he expelled the air, it came out as a visible puff, reminding him of when they were young. They'd pretend to be dragons and blow out long breaths as they ran in the yard. Neither wanted to be the knight. No, they both wanted to be the destroyer.

"Legend tells of a curse brought to these lands by the first king—"

"King Harald," Sigurd said, getting a nod from Johan.

"Yes, Harald Fairhair. It is said that he visited these very trees during one of his campaigns—one of his last, in fact. He lived into his eighties, you know."

"I do," Sigurd replied, "everyone in all of Norway knows of King Harald, but what does he have to do with this?" He motioned to the woods around them.

"Quit interrupting me and I'll tell you!" Johan snapped, his deep thunderous voice echoing around them. Then he grinned, getting an angry look out of his brother. Even in such a stressful time, Johan couldn't help but tease his sibling. It was a way for him to keep calm when inside the damned forest, a feat not easily accomplished. Sigurd, however, appeared unconcerned.

Because he doesn't believe… Yet.

Johan continued. "Very little is known about our king's life after he unified our homeland. Yes, there are many stories about him, but most are thought to be romantic tales and nothing more, just overstated fictions." He again drew a long breath, blowing it out hard. "But what some think really happened is that he found something out in the wilds—something that changed the course of his life."

"This sounds like one of those 'overstated fictions', Johan."

He nodded. "Quite so, but there's always truth in even the silliest of comedies. Lessons that need to be learned and applied."

Sigurd knew he was right about that, it was something their father used to say. "Go on."

"Right…" Johan said, starting their hike again. "While famous for bonding Norway into one land, Fairhair was also known for something else."

"And what is that?" Sigurd asked.

"He was obsessed with the gods of old, and with possessing their magic and power."

"Gods of old? You mean Odin and Thor."

"Indeed," Johan replied. "Fairhair believed the mythology to be true, so much so, that he would routinely search for relics of the time during his various campaigns. He kept the findings, if any, private, only divulging what he found to other true believers within his closest circle."

Sigurd's eyes widen. "You're one of them, aren't you? A believer in the old ways."

Johan simply nodded, silently answering his brother's inquiry. He'd been a follower for nearly twenty years, but this was the first time he'd ever dared reveal it to his brother. "We're almost there."

"Almost where?" Sigurd asked.

Johan pulled a small book from his pocket, showing it to Sigurd. There was a symbol branded into its simple leather cover, a symbol Sigurd recognized.

"Is that a *valknut*?"

Johan held up the small tome. It was most definitely the famous three triangle symbol. The word literally meant "slain warriors knot." This one had been altered slightly, however. In addition to the three interlocking triangles, there was also a single staff passing through the links horizontally. Everyone in the region knew of it. They also knew what it signified.

"Odin?" Sigurd asked.

"Yes," Johan replied, turning the book upside down, "and no."

Sigurd saw the book was *now* right-side up.

"An inverted valknut? What does it mean?"

"As you know," Johan explained, "the traditional valknut symbolizes a warrior's passing and also that of Odin's power over that specific death. It is said that Odin could raise those from the dead that were given this symbol on their tombs."

"I've never heard the second part of that before."

Johan smiled. "Believe me, brother, it's true."

"And the inversion?" Sigurd asked, letting Johan's cryptic answer slide.

"It symbolizes the curse—"

"A curse?"

"Yes. Some of us believe there is an ancient curse upon this land. Something belonging to the gods is buried here."

"Don't tell me you actually believe those stories."

"I wouldn't expect you to understand, brother. But you know, even if you won't admit it, that there is a sickness here. Promise me brother, if we find what is damning these lands, be careful and do not lay your hands upon it."

"Find what? What are you talking about? Who are these people you've gotten yourself involved with?"

"Protectors of a secret knowledge that goes back to the time of King Harald himself. It seems our greatest fear has been realized."

"And what's that?"

"That whatever Fairhair found here, he eventually put back."

"What did he supposedly find?"

Sigurd watched as his brother's normally unemotional face creased in worry. Johan didn't spook easily. Something out here scared him and that alone terrified Sigurd.

"If what this book says is true, then we are getting close. After years of searching…"

"*Years?*"

Johan didn't finish the thought, but instead resumed walking. "Follow me,"

They continued in silence for another twenty minutes. Johan stayed far enough ahead of his brother to keep them from having to speak. Sigurd did not press his brother for more information. He wanted their time together to be civil. They didn't get to do things like this very often anymore.

They entered a small clearing and found no path to follow. Either it didn't exist or….

"Which way?" Sigurd asked.

Johan flipped to a page in the back of his book, and then pointed to the northwest. He cautiously approached a thicket of low growing shrubs and pushed them aside to reveal another footpath just beyond, but instead of it being made of natural earth, the newfound trail was paved with cut stone.

"What is this place?" Sigurd asked, stepping through first.

"This path leads to the *Resting Grounds.*"

"A cemetery?"

"A tomb." Johan said reverently. "The tomb of Harald Fairhair."

"King Harald's tomb is here?" Sigurd asked. According to traditional lore, the king was buried in a mound in Haugesund, more than a hundred miles to the east. "But if that's true, it would be the discovery of a lifetime. Why haven't you told anyone? People need to know about this."

"Not this. The curse hangs heaviest here."

"Enough, Johan!" Sigurd shouted, his voice echoing around them. Johan cringed at the sound. Sigurd must have noticed, for his demeanor softened. "Forgive me. I know this is important to you."

Johan looked deep into his brother's eyes, doing what he could to hide the fear in his own. "Come *bror*, I will show you."

"Show me what?" Sigurd asked, heading down the trail. The footpath itself was the only unnatural thing before them. They were nearly ten miles outside of town and hadn't seen another living soul for some time. Even the wildlife in the area was oddly sparse.

"Show me what, Johan?" Sigurd asked again, frustration ringing in his voice.

Johan glanced back at him, unable to articulate the fear he felt.

They moved in silence for ten minutes, following the inclining path further and further to the northwest. It seemed to get colder with each passing minute, but Sigurd knew it was just a combination of the anticipation and exhaustion.

Except us. Sigurd tried his best to ignore his own apprehension.

The path banked out of sight around to the left, causing Johan to slow a bit. Mirroring his brother's movements, Sigurd did the same. It was not until Johan drew his large axe that he questioned his brother's sanity.

"What are you doing?"

"Being careful."

About what? Sigurd asked himself. He was finished asking his brother any questions for now. All Johan's *answers* did was lead to more queries.

The path narrowed, forcing Sigurd to fall in line behind Johan. Both Larsens were larger than average, giants to some, standing nearly a head taller than most men. They, like their father and grandfather before them, were each thick and powerfully built, and because of it, the only thing Sigurd could see was the back of Johan's broad shoulders.

And his thick skull, thought Sigurd.

Whatever lay ahead of them was still a mystery.

Until, Johan stepped aside....

The path ended at a black iron gate set right into the side of the mountain. The metal was so dark that Sigurd could only describe the color as *evil*. The small amount of light that penetrated the canopy above didn't reflect off its surface. The natural light absorbed into it like it was being consumed.

With great care, Johan opened the gate. Beyond lay the yawning darkness of a cavern. He picked up a large rotted tree branch lying nearby and tied a cloth around the end of the branch, creating a makeshift torch, which he lit with a matchstick, and then stepped into the opening. He looked back to his brother and nodded. Sigurd returned the nod and started forward, following close behind, gripping his own axe.

They traveled for a few minutes, deeper into the rock. The path dipped slightly, beckoning them further, and eventually bringing them to the mouth of a natural cave, much larger than anything either man had seen before. At its center was a raised coffin, black as night just like the gate. Surrounding it was a flowing mound of treasure—coins and jewels. It was truly a king's wealth.

But when Johan lowered the torch the wavering firelight revealed only death.

The cave was full of bodies, long-dead judging by the rot. The only thing left was bone and whatever clothing they had worn. Sigurd breathed a silent prayer as they stepped further into the mass grave, tiptoeing carefully around them.

The number of carcasses wasn't what caught Sigurd's attention but rather their size. They were larger than even he and Johan—true giants, monsters from the depths of Hell. The bones were thicker than a man's, powerfully built. Though human in shape, the skulls had long canines, like fangs, and the hands and feet curled into talons.

"What were they?" Sigurd gasped.

Johan turned and faced him. "They were us, Sigurd. They were men cursed. The king sought this secret for over fifty years, and unfortunately for him, he found it. It's said to give the man who wields it unlimited power… But at great cost."

"What was buried with Fairhair?" Sigurd asked, sweating despite the cool dank air in the cave.

Johan held up the journal again showing Sigurd the insignia. "Look closer," he said. Sigurd did and saw that it wasn't just a staff within the valknut. It had a pointed end and looked just like a…

"A spear," Sigurd said, mystified.

Johan turned and made his way to the coffin, putting his weight against its lid. At first, it didn't budge, but

Johan grunted and began to move it. It wasn't until Sigurd joined in, that they finally shoved it aside. The jet-black lid crashed to the floor, revealing the dead king in full battle armor. Clutched in his lifeless hands was a spear, black as obsidian and as tall as Sigurd himself.

"*Gungnir,*" Johan whispered in awe. "The favored weapon of Odin, the *Allfather*, king of the gods."

Johan reached for the fabled spear, but Sigurd held out a restraining hand. "Don't, brother. This doesn't feel right."

Johan ignored him

Sigurd desperately tried to hold back his brother, but Johan thrust a thick, powerful elbow into his face, knocking him to the ground. With a manic expression, he seized the weapon.

Holding his bloodied nose, Sigurd could see runes inscribed into the blade and shaft—runes he recognized but didn't comprehend.

The language of the gods, perhaps.

Johan began to growl. His grunts quickly turned into screams about a curse—*the* curse. Backing away, Sigurd watched in astonishment as Johan began to change.

Johan lurched forward. *Gungnir* fell from his grip, returning to the forsaken coffin, landing on Fairhair's chest. Johan gripped the crypt's edge and howled into the air.

He sounded like he was dying.

Sigurd recoiled at the sound of cracking bones and at the sight of his brother's skin stretching and tearing. Johan's coat and shirt split apart as his bulk grew, revealing a pelt of gray fur sprouting from his back and shoulders.

Sigurd knew he should've been running, but he

couldn't. The sight of his only brother turning into a beast rendered him too terrified to move.

As Johan turned toward Sigurd, his face began to elongate. His eyes changed from their normal steel-blue to a sickening blood-red. His appearance was exactly that of the bodies around them. He looked human enough but had turned into what Sigurd knew was something much worse than a *man*.

His brother was in the grip of the legendary *berserkergang*.

Tears flowed down Sigurd's face and he crossed himself, praying for the nightmare to end.

Lost in a primal bloodlust, Johan swept a dagger-tipped hand at his brother.

Sigurd dove between Johan's legs and scrambled around to the opposite side of the coffin but could not avoid being raked by Johan's claws. The wounds were deep. He could feel his blood flowing free and fast, soaking his clothes in seconds.

Knowing his life was near its end, and not seeing another way out, Sigurd did the only thing that he knew could stop the monstrous Johan. "I'm sorry, *bror*," he whispered, and then reached into the coffin and took hold of *Gungnir*. He screamed as something snapped in his mind, then, he too began to transform into one of Odin's bestial warriors.

He would kill Johan, and in return, he prayed his brother did the same to him.

ONE

The creature stared him down, intent on making him its next meal.

"Being a wolf's lunch wasn't what I had planned for today," Torbjorn Sorensen mumbled to himself, but if he wasn't careful, he might just be.

Sorensen loved hiking into the wilderness surrounding the town, camping, sometimes for days on end. It was the only thing that could quiet his mind thoroughly that didn't include alcohol.

He had enough of that in his younger days.

The peace of the outdoors was something he couldn't get enough of, and like his great-grandfather, Johan Larsen, "Tor" would've rather just built a cabin away from civilization and called it a career. Instead, he had become a schoolteacher.

Like most children in the 21st century, his students didn't want to be in school any more than he did. He *loved* history, he lived for it. But after twenty-five years of doing the work, his soul craved something else, which was why he'd decided to spend his holiday break tramping through the wilderness, and why he now found himself facing a hungry gray wolf.

Guns weren't permitted in the woods without a hunting license, and even if he had one, it wasn't open season. Regardless, he never thought he needed one. It didn't mean he wasn't *armed*, though. He was not however, by any means, unarmed.

He slowly reached back and gripped the handle of the oversized splitting axe protruding from his pack. He often bragged that it was the sharpest in Norway. He'd won multiple outdoorsmen trophies with it over the years. Now in his late forties, he was, by almost a decade, the oldest to enter the annual competition yet, he had won three out of the last four.

The second weapon was the *storbukken* knife his father had carried during his military service. The stout six-inch blade wasn't frightful looking, but like his axe, it was sharp—the *second sharpest* blade in Norway.

At six-foot-seven, Sorensen towered over the wolf, but the gray wolf had something he didn't: An untamable killer instinct.

While imposing in size, Sorensen was a gentle soul at heart. He never hunted and had flatly refused to do so. Killing for sustenance seemed unnecessarily primitive and taking a creature's life in the name of sport was abhorrent.

"I'll kill you if I have to," he said, speaking calmly to the snarling predator. "But maybe this can end better for both of us."

It stood twenty feet from him, head lowered, lips peeled back in a sneer. Why it was out here alone without its pack, he wasn't sure. Maybe it had challenged the pack leader and lost. Sometimes, when that happened, the loser was cast out, forced to wander the wilds alone.

He looked hungry, too. Sorensen could see its ribs

He took a step back, hoping the wolf would let him flee if he didn't provoke it. Unfortunately, it didn't, but took a step forward, matching him. Its paw sank into the snow, reminding Sorensen that his footing would be sloppy. His confidence would be stronger if he was on solid ground.

He knew that if he could get to his backpack, he could toss the starving animal a few pieces of jerky he'd picked up in town. Unfortunately, that would mean letting go of his axe.

Maybe, just maybe, he could lose it in the thicker trees behind him to the north. It was the exact opposite direction that he wanted to go but he'd trade dying for returning late to town any day.

"*Dra til helvete*," he said, cursing at the animal.

He backed away slowly, knowing better than to turn his back on the wolf, occasionally swinging the axe before him to remind the creature that he had a long reach. Thankfully, there was packed snow closer to the woods, and patches of dry ground under the trees. As soon as he reached them, he turned and ran.

Snarling erupted from behind, causing him to weave in and out of the populating growth. He took a few branches across his face but paid the small cuts no attention. If he slowed at all, he'd have some much larger wounds to deal with.

He cut back and forth between the trees at random intervals. As he leaped a felled tree, he glanced over his shoulder and found the wolf practically at his heels, running silent. Abandoning his plan, Sorensen ducked around the next tree and held his axe at the ready, backing into a small clearing as he did.

The attack was so sudden, he didn't have time to prepare.

The wolf leaped straight for his throat, fangs bared. The only thing Sorensen could think to do was hold the axe's long, ash handle out to block the gaping jaws and take the brunt of the impact with his body. He did exactly that as the wolf bulled into him, tackling him to the ground. He pushed the axe handle into the wolf's maw and locked out his elbows, giving himself a *comfortable* buffer between his face and the powerful jaws. But he couldn't hold the thing off forever.

Leaning back, he jammed his booted feet up and into the beast's belly, kicking with all his might, and flung the enraged animal over his head. The wolf crashed into the thicket but recovered quickly and moved in for another attack.

Leaping to his feet, Sorensen gripped the haft of his axe in both hands and raised it above his head. He didn't want to kill the wolf, but he knew it would never give up. When the wolf charged again, he did not hold back.

The blow landed with such force that it twisted the axe out of his grip. The animal let out a truncated squeal, and then collapsed.

Sorensen fell to his knees before it, tears already streaming down his face, and drew his knife. If the creature still clung to life, he would have to cut its throat. But there was no need. The blow from the axe had split its skull nearly in two.

He returned the knife to its sheath and reached for the axe. As he did, he spotted something curious in the tree line. Where the wolf's fall had trampled the brush, he saw what looked like a path.

The life and death struggle slipped from his mind as he took a cautious step toward the opening. Where the snow had been swept away by the disturbance, he saw dark gray stones, laid out to form a path.

No one knew the history of the region better than he, and yet this was something even he had never heard of.

He moved forward, clearing the path through the trees with his axe.

After clearing several such entanglements, the path brought him to the base of a cliff covered with dry brambles. He cleared these away to reveal a shadowy opening in the stone.

Overcome with curiosity, he paused just long enough to take his flashlight from his pack. He clicked it on and entered. Inside was a tunnel just large enough for him to fit without having to turn sideways. He continued unperturbed for a few minutes eventually passing into a large chamber.

It reminded him of Kivik Kungagraven—the King's Grave—in the south of Sweden. The tomb was one of the largest stone graves of the era, sitting a thousand feet from the Baltic shore. But this tomb was different in that it was naturally formed and in a mountain. Its ceiling was covered in stalactites, some even attaching to stalagmites, forming beautifully-ancient columns.

It wasn't until he took his eyes off the ceiling and examined the cave itself that he understood what he'd found.

The chamber was occupied.

Bodies—pieces of them really—lay strewn about. He knelt to examine something that looked like a hand and forearm. Even stripped of flesh, it was easily twice the size of his own.

"Giants," he whispered.

He stood and played his light across the field of monstrous remains. Something glittered in the darkness—an unimaginable wealth of gold and gemstones—and yet rather than elation, Sorensen felt a profound disquiet. Directly ahead, on a raised bier, was a coffin, its lid ajar and leaning to one side.

Warily, he moved toward it, and as he did, he stepped over two bodies that looked much fresher than the rest. They were not the remains of men, but rather of beasts. One had its jaws wrapped around the other's throat. The other impaled its foe with two sets of razor-sharp claws. Yet, they appeared to be wearing clothing.

"What are you?" Sorensen asked, kneeling beside one of them. He spotted something under it—a small book, bound in leather. He carefully extracted it and brought it into the light.

There was an odd symbol pressed into its cover, a valknut, but with something like a spear passing through it.

His eyes widened in disbelief. Shaking with fear, he got to his feet and approached the coffin.

It was there, just as he knew it would be.

"Gungnir," he whispered. "It's real. God help us all."

TWO

Key West, Florida

Dane Maddock sat on the deck of his condominium, eyes closed, letting the sun kiss his skin, deepening his tan. He knew better than to fall asleep in direct sunlight, but he also knew that the sun would set over the Gulf of Mexico long before sunburn became a concern. He lingered in a sort of half-awake state, hovering just above slumber. But then his phone rang, shattering the blissful peace of his almost-nap. Groaning, he opened his eyes, blinking awake, and glanced at the device's screen. He groaned again, seeing an unlisted number.

Begrudgingly, he answered. "This is Maddock."

"Hello, Dane."

Maddock sat up quickly at hearing the voice. "Tam, hi. What's up?" A call from Tam Broderick could go one of several ways: interesting, exciting, annoying, dangerous, or some combination thereof. In any case, he owed her a few favors and she wasn't shy about calling them in.

"I need your help with something." Tamara Broderick, leader of the Myrmidon Squad, an arm of the CIA, was never one to beat around the bush. This phone call wasn't an exception either.

Completely awake now, Maddock stood. Whenever Tam needed his team's help it was serious. And dangerous.

"I'm listening," Maddock said, quickly guzzling down a bottle of water as she spoke.

"We intercepted a message from a small town in

Norway earlier in the week. Apparently, there was an archaeological discovery made up in the mountains north of Vikersund. We need you to take a *careful* look."

Careful? So, it's off-the-books then….

"Why us?" Maddock asked unsure why he was contacted in the first place.

"You owe me."

He sighed. Tam kept scrupulous track of favors owed. "That's not what I asked. Why us, specifically?"

"ScanoGen is involved."

"ScanoGen?" Maddock asked. ScanoGen was a biotech company with whom Maddock and his crew had crossed paths a few times in the past. "Wait, I'm confused, Tam. I didn't know they were still in play. Besides, I thought they were more interested in exotic botanicals than archaeological discoveries?"

"I'm getting there. The man who found the site sent out a chain email to some colleagues of his, asking some strange questions. The verbiage was odd too, like he couldn't choose his words. Weird for a man with his education and reputation. We picked up on it when we flagged a few choice words."

"And those are?"

"Legend. Death. Treasure. Creatures. Weapon," Tam said, listing them off.

"Oh, well, that would do it then, wouldn't it?"

"It would," she replied. "Seems to be right up your alley I'd say."

Maddock rubbed his face with his free hand and thought. A hush-hush mission meant a small team, if any *team* at all. Bones would most definitely accompany him. *What of the others?*

Tam answered the question.

"Just you and Bones on this one. Vikersund is a beautiful, little, out-of-the-way town on the southwest bank of Lake Tyri. Too many outsiders would send up red flags everywhere. ScanoGen may already be in route and we need to get you there first. And if they beat you there, we need you to arrive unnoticed."

Not really knowing what to say and realizing she was right about them owing her, Maddock capitulated. "Okay, Tam, you win."

"Good…" He heard something coming in low and loud, his shoulders slumping as he did, "Because we're outside waiting."

Even as she said it, Maddock heard the roar of a jet engine. The air was suddenly filled with a deep, rhythmic vibration. He turned and ran inside the condo to the front windows, threw aside the curtains and saw it. Fifty yards away, in the center of the street, hovering not twenty feet off the ground, was an unmarked black helicopter.

His hand fell away from the side of his face as the aircraft turned and the side door opened. A familiar form—a female one—edged out and stood, one foot on the landing strut. She wore khaki trousers and a black T-shirt, both of which nicely accentuated her curvy figure. A headset outfitted with a lip mic covered her ears. Her chocolate brown face was split with a big toothy grin.

He brought the phone back up to his ear. "What if I said no?"

She laughed. "You *never* say no."

So, what exactly are we going after?" Bones asked, tying his hair back in its customary ponytail. The rotor wash of the helicopter had messed it up upon entering the rear hold. Satisfied with his work, he leaned back against the uncomfortable seat. He'd sat in relative silence since take off, waiting for Tam to further explain their mission.

Not one to keep his mouth shut for too long, the large Native American was still trying to wake up, yawning every few minutes. After his fifth such yawn, Tam took exception to the act.

"Are we boring you, Uriah?" she asked. If she was trying to get under his skin, using his given name would work.

Bones leaned forward, looking hard at the brown-skinned beauty. "First of all, *girl*, don't call me that." He winked. *Willis would be proud.* "Secondly, yes, you bore me big time."

"Lord Jesus give me strength," Tam said, rubbing her forehead, squeezing her eyes shut.

He grinned and glanced at Maddock, getting a scowl in return. Bones held up his hands in surrender and sat back, motioning for Tam to continue.

"Go ahead," Maddock said.

Tam nodded a thank you and did. "As I said earlier, an email was sent speaking of a tomb that, as far as we know, doesn't exist. There is no account of anything in any historical records we have."

"Whose tomb is it?" Maddock asked.

She shrugged. "No idea. That's what we're hoping you can find out when you get boots on the ground. All we know is that it has something to do with an ancient king of the region."

"I imagine there's a few of those," Maddock said, not liking the lack of specificity. Tam was normally much more prepared than this. "Anything else, or are we shooting from the hip on this one?"

"There's one more thing." She dug into her pack and pulled out a folded sheet of paper. Handing it to Maddock, she explained what it was.

"The only other thing in the message was this symbol. The emailer, a man named Torbjorn Sorenson, asked a few of his contemporaries to check into it. While well-versed in Viking lore himself, Sorensen seems to have some friends at a few of the larger Norwegian universities that are even deeper into it than him."

"What is it?" Bones asked as Maddock unfolded it and looked.

Maddock knew what one of them was. It was a common knot used in many cultures.

But what does the spear mean?

"This, my friends," Tam said, "is a little-known symbol belonging to the Norse god, Odin, or rather his weapon of choice, a spear named—"

"Gungnir," Maddock finished. "I know it."

"Gung-what?" Bones asked, lost.

"Gungnir," Maddock replied. "It was Odin's lance and said to be mightier than Thor's hammer, *Mjolnir*."

"Ah, yes, Thor," Bones said.

"Not the superhero," Tam added getting a frown from Bones.

"Are you telling me that this Sorensen guy found Odin's spear?" Maddock asked.

"We aren't sure, but he seems to think so."

Maddock nodded thinking. Something else was bothering him about this. "What about the creatures from the email. What does that have to do with this?"

She leaned forward. "Have you heard of the berserkers?"

"Like Wolverine going *berserker* on people?"

quipped Bones.

No answer.

"Never mind," he said, sitting back again.

"I thought the Norse berserkers were just crazy Viking warriors sent in first as *shock troops*," Maddock said. "They supposedly got massively intoxicated before battles. Some were even said to use a narcotic of some sort. Either way, they fought without feeling pain or backing down. They literally went 'berserk.'"

Tam didn't answer. Her normal stoic expression actually looked nervous.

"What is it?" Maddock asked.

"Sorensen seemed frightened by what he found. Unfortunately, he didn't go into any further detail." She leaned on her knees. "I think he may have found something far worse than just a bunch of dead drunken Vikings and a spear."

"Sounds like the first thing we need to do is talk to this Sorensen guy," Bones said, re-entering the conversation. "There's a reason he didn't mention more, I'd guess."

"Why do you say that?" Tam asked.

"Why wouldn't he mention it if it *wasn't* something terrible?" he replied. "Where's the harm in it if you've already gone to all the trouble of writing the damn message in the first place."

Maddock nodded, staring off into space, thinking. "He's right. Our first stop needs to be Sorensen. We need to know what else he found."

Again, Tam was quiet.

"Your silence is never good for us, you know that?" Bones laughed as the aircraft bounced beneath them. Being a former SEAL, like Maddock, the bucking of a helo could eventually rock him to sleep like a baby in a swing.

Maddock didn't speak. He just waited for Tam to continue. He didn't want to verbally agree with Bones again. His big friend was right, but he didn't want it to go to his head.

"Sorensen went missing yesterday morning," she finally said.

"Told you," Bones said, rubbing his temples.

"He didn't show up for work this morning and no one has seen him since the night before. He's regarded as overly punctual, especially when it comes to his teaching career. The students love him and he never misses a class."

"What about his family?" Maddock asked.

"None to speak of," she replied, pulling a file from her backpack.

Maddock flipped it open. It was the portfolio of one, Torbjorn Johan Sorensen. He was a history major from a school Maddock couldn't pronounce, in a city and county he also couldn't pronounce. It seemed that Sorensen was also handy with a splitting axe. A local legend of sorts.

Small town people….

"Something spooked him," Maddock mumbled, getting Bones' attention. "Something made him go underground."

"ScanoGen?" Tam asked, trying to think of what could've scared the man so badly. "Maybe he got wind of people coming for him?"

"Or whatever he found in the forest," Bones added, getting a nod from Maddock.

"Regardless," Maddock said, "we need to tread softly.

Best case scenario is that ScanoGen never hears of our involvement."

THREE

Vikersund, Norway

"So, this is Vikersund?" Bones asked, his eyes taking in the snow-topped peaks that ringed the quaint mountain town. Vikersund was the definition of a small town, barely having 3,000 people living within its borders. "I feel like a bull in a china shop around here."

"I'm not sure what that's supposed to mean," Maddock commented, smiling. "Are you gonna go around and smash the place up or something? Because if you are—"

"Screw you," Bones retorted, walking away. "I'm blaming you if Kathy Bates comes at me with a sledgehammer." Two steps later, he stopped and looked back, getting down to business. "Where do we start?"

Maddock stood in the center of town and had a look around. He unconsciously adjusted the watch Tam had given them upon landing. It looked like a simple *Apple Watch* but, in reality, it was a high-tech piece of spy gear. Its GPS system was better than anything else on the planet and it had a direct line back to Tam. She and a small team were holed up in a hotel in the next town over. If things went south and they needed a quick EVAC, they could do it with ease.

They were in a small clearing surrounded by a circular street, lined with locally owned businesses. Most were of the standard variety: outdoor sports equipment, a grocery store, a hardware store. Remembering that Sorensen was a champion with an axe, Maddock pointed to the sports store.

"Let's start there."

The two men walked across the empty street and as they did, Maddock noticed a lone figure standing on the street corner, picking at his fingernail with a small pocket knife. Pulling open the door, Maddock smiled when he looked up and saw an old-fashioned doorbell ding overhead. *The simple things.* He let Bones enter first and paused for a moment and watched the stranger. Only once did the black-haired man look up, and when he did, he locked eyes with Maddock and smiled. After an uncomfortable pause, he nodded a polite hello and went back to work on his cuticles.

Huh, he thought, but shook his head. They had no enemies in Vikersund. *Is ScanoGen already here?*

Halfway in the store, Maddock leaned back out and saw that the stranger was gone. He looked up and down the main road but found it empty. It was midday and most everyone in town was working.

Except whoever that was.

He shook his head again and entered the business. Two checkout counters were positioned dead center, just inside the door, and behind them, the rest of the store was filled with rows of equipment. They carried everything from fishing gear to—of course—axes. The entire left-hand wall was covered in them—floor to ceiling—like how some gun stores in the States looked. He wondered if Vikersund actually had a gun dealer. It really didn't matter since Tam had gotten them into Norway with their sidearms without a hitch, but in the unlikely event that they needed an ammunition resupply, it would be nice to know where to go. Both of them wore holsters positioned at the small of their backs, concealed by their large winter coats. It was so cold and their jackets so thick that they both could've probably carried shotguns, too.

"*Velkommen, kan eg hjelpe deg?*"

Maddock turned and found Bones attempting to converse with a local.

"Dude, do you speak any English?" Bones asked.

"Yes, some," the shopkeeper replied, smiling.

"Good deal," Bones mumbled, elbowing Maddock as he approached. "You're up."

Maddock took over the questioning. "Torbjorn Sorensen, you know him?"

The man nodded. "Champion." He motioned to a wall where a tall, strong man held a massive axe on one shoulder. He stood like Captain Morgan with one leg up on a tree stump. His face was in a few of the pictures.

"We were hoping to interview him for our online show," Maddock said, holding out his hand. "My name is Mike Jagger and this is my partner, Keith Richardson." They both held out their false credentials sporting duplicate ESPN logos.

"I'm sorry," the clerk said, "I don't know where Tor is."

Maddock smiled his thanks and asked to look around. The shopkeeper looked pleased for the potential business and emphatically nodded. They still needed to find Sorensen before ScanoGen did and decided that staying in the warmth of the shop for the time being was better than the cold of the outside. Maddock preferred the warmth of the Keys. He knew Bones felt the same way, maybe even more so. The bitter cold was something only a lunatic or a polar bear would choose to live in.

The front door dinged for the first time since they entered, announcing the arrival of another patron.

Maddock was immediately on guard. Something in the back of Maddock's brain couldn't let go of the man on the street corner. Something about him was off.

"Move!" Maddock hissed, pushing the much-larger Bones deeper into the store and then behind the endcap between rows five and six.

"What are you—"

"Shhh," Maddock warned, finger over his lips.

Slowly both men peeked out, one to each side of the endcap. Maddock wasn't at all surprised to see the stranger, along with two other men, saunter in like they owned the joint. The other two newcomers were almost the size of Bones while the stranger was around Maddock's height and build give-or-take an inch and ten pounds.

"This can't be good," Bones mumbled, leaning back behind the endcap. "I'm guessing these guys are here for us."

"Whatever gave you that idea?" Maddock asked sarcastically. He was stunned at how fast they got to Vikersund. "Whatever Sorensen found, must be pretty important to them."

Could it really be Gungnir—the 'real' Gungnir? Maddock knew one thing, ScanoGen didn't show up for artifacts unless there was something else about them that aligned with their own goals. An old spear meant little to them unless it held a darker secret. The secretive biotech company loved *bio*logics, especially the ones with the potential to destroy life. Those went for the highest price. ScanoGen navigated the business world without a moral compass and sold death and destruction to anyone who could meet their asking price.

"How are we doing this?" Bones asked, glancing

down to the shorter Maddock. At six-six, Bones literally looked down on most everyone, even his partner who was almost six-feet-tall himself. He reached around the small of his back and drew his Glock.

"Quietly," Maddock replied, pushing Bones' gun down. "We need to keep our cover intact. It's a small town and two outsiders with guns will be easy to spot later on. But two regular Joes just defending themselves…"

Growling, Bones holstered the pistol. "Fine, but no promises I ain't messing up the place."

Maddock didn't answer. He peeked around the endcap once more and saw the stranger standing just inside the door. The other two men were gone, however.

Probably looking for us.

Tapping Bones on the shoulder, Maddock motioned for him to go right. He then made a circular motion with his finger and pointed to the front door. They'd meet there when finished.

Nodding, Bones moved off and headed for the first aisle while Maddock moved toward the last. There were a total of ten rows of goods, separated by freestanding shelving units. As he moved down the back aisle, Maddock noticed the place had a backdoor they could use if needed.

He was almost to the rear right corner of the store when he saw something he could use for self-defense if it came to that. The signage was all in Norwegian, a language neither he nor Bones spoke or read, but the object itself was one he'd seen many times.

In the States, they were called *King Kooker* stirring paddles and resembled a smaller wooden canoe oar. It was sturdy and would do nicely in a fight. Plus, if his plan worked out like he hoped, Maddock would be able to stroll down the aisle with it over his shoulder, doing his best to seem unintimidating and clueless.

Oar in hand, Maddock leisurely rounded the corner and spotted a large, but thankfully, unarmed man. Doing his best not to look the other guy's direction, he continued forward. Acting like a shopper, he flicked his head back and forth, pretending to be engrossed in the store's wares.

But he wasn't.

Maddock was formulating what to do with the stranger once he got through with this one. It looked like a close-quarters brawl was his in future, something Maddock actually preferred.

Then, the man decided to ruin his plan by grabbing a large machete.

Damn.

Gripping his paddle harder, Maddock felt its solid construction. He knew the wood could take a beating and hopefully he could use its three-foot-length to his advantage. Staying out of the hulking man's reach would be ideal.

Easily bigger than Bones, the bald man was a bull, thick and powerful where it mattered most. Maddock was pretty good in a fight but relied more on his wits than raw power. Whether that gave him the advantage or not was something only combat would reveal.

When they were ten feet away from one another, the other man's eyes narrowed and he launched his attack.

FOUR

While Maddock was no doubt strategically planning his upcoming fight, Bones was going to just bull rush the other guy and see what happened. Unfortunately for him, his opponent thought the same.

Sprinting out from behind the endcap, he was startled by the man waiting for him, arms outstretched. Even with his own impressive size, Bones was still very agile and ducked as something *whooshed* over his head. He turned the maneuver into a coordinated roll and came up on his feet, fists up.

"Crap…"

The *thing* that buzzed the top of his head was a very large, very sharp-looking axe. He glanced to his left and saw that the entire aisle was full of woodcutting implements—everything from hatchets to chainsaws.

"Geez," he muttered, "I thought sporting goods meant they sold golf clubs."

He scrambled back out of reach and considered going for his gun, but before he could, he bumped into a hip-high display table. When he saw what was on it, he smiled.

Hatchets.

Bones grabbed two of them, one for each hand, and twirled them expertly, grinning from ear to ear. He paused and looked over his opponent. The guy was roughly the same size as him, but much thicker around the waist. Bones was lean for his size. This guy was a real bear of a man.

The axe attack came faster than expected. Bones leaned away from the blow, parrying with both hatchet blades. A resounding *clang* rang out through the store, alerting everyone to what was happening. Maddock was no doubt having a go at it with the other guy, but Bones couldn't worry about him.

He had his own problems to deal with.

The reverberating metal stung his ears, and he flinched. The reaction saved his life as he tripped and fell head over heels onto, and then over, the table. As soon as he hit the ground, he rolled backward, anticipating another attack.

A sharp crack rang out as the assassin's axe head smashed through the display, obliterating it. Bringing the weapon high over his head again, the attacker went for the killing blow, but instead, Bones used that brief unguarded moment to go on the offensive.

Immediately after finishing his back roll, he planted his feet into the ground and dove forward, launching himself into the would-be killer. He'd left the hatchets on the floor. Instead of using the unfamiliar weapons, he'd use his two most trusted ones: His fists. His shoulder met the other guy's exposed stomach, bowling him back into a large, immovable shelf of equipment. More things went flying as Bones spun the guy around, driving him into another display of tools.

Two massive hands came down on Bones' neck, loosening his grip enough to be pried away and tossed aside. He slammed into a rack of gloves and wide-brimmed fishing hats, one of the latter comically flopping on his head. Paying it no attention, he stood and balled his fists, connecting with a hard jab to the guy's jaw. Then, he laid into him with a second shot, followed by a hard right cross which broke the man's nose. Bones kicked him in the stomach and, as the man staggered backward, knocked him off his feet with an uppercut that Ryu from *Street Fighter* would've been proud of.

Breathing hard, he watched as the other guy slowly got to his feet. "Holy crap, dude, do us both a favor and stay down!" Bones let fly with another strong right but was shocked when the bloodied man caught his fist with one hand and grinned.

"Aw, crap," Bones muttered.

The man yanked Bones forward, headbutting him with the force of a mule kick. Stars danced in his vision. Teetering back, his wobbling legs won the battle. He stumbled backward, flipping over another table. Landing awkwardly, he rolled over and pushed up to hands and knees, breathing hard. Then, without even knowing why, he reached up and pulled the fishing hat down tighter on his head.

He grabbed the first thing within reach—a small rubber mallet, probably meant for pounding tent stakes—and chucked it at his foe. The mallet went sailing through the air only to bounce harmlessly off the other guy's chest. He'd need more than that to take *big boy* out. He thought about going for his gun but still felt woozy from the headbutt.

No guns... Civilians....

He grabbed another, larger mallet, aimed lower, and hurled it. The hammer struck right on target.

"Bam!" Bones chortled, and then in a passable impression of the Swedish Chef from the Muppets added. "Right in the dingle-hopper."

Grunting from the blow, the guy bent over and grabbed himself. Bones used the man's posture against him. He leaped onto a third table and jumped straight into the air, bringing his elbow down on the back of his skull. The man went down in a heap but immediately started to scrape himself off the floor.

Not a chance!

Bones lashed out with his foot as hard as he could, connecting with the side of the man's head. The fight finally went out of him and he collapsed, unconscious.

His head still swimming, Bones could only think of one thing.

Maddock.

In no rush to get his face beat in, Maddock used a much more thought out approach to his own fight. He kept the guy in front of him guessing while poking at him with his longer-range *weapon*. In reality, he was just trying to annoy the guy into making a mistake and give him an opening.

Maddock jabbed at the man's face and then his stomach. Once or twice he went for a shot below the belt. Every time he attacked, the other man reacted and parried him away. And, with every parry, chips of wood flew from Maddock's oar. It was beginning to look like a serrated knife blade. If he kept it up, pretty soon Maddock would have a passable thrusting spear.

But the man was clearly wearying of the game. He slashed harder and more often, breathing heavier with every blow. Maddock was tiring him out, playing Rocky to this man's Drago.

Wear him down and then strike.

The much bigger man tried two successive attacks, flailing wildly with the second. Maddock took the opening, spun the paddle around, shoving the handle's thick, knobbed end into the man's face, hitting him squarely in the left eye. The man howled in pain and aggravation, his eye squeezed shut and streaming tears. Maddock retreated a few steps and waited for the uncoordinated, anger-fueled reprisal.

It never came.

Instead, the machete-wielding mountain backed away and drew a small caliber pistol, intent on ending Maddock's games once and for all. Eyes wide, and on the wrong side of a gun barrel, Maddock darted forward and jabbed the splintered end of the paddle into the gunman's wrist. Shouting, the brute dropped the pistol, giving Maddock the opening he desired.

Kicking out, Maddock caught the inside of the man's right knee, buckling his leg. Next, he brought the flat part of the paddle up into his foe's chin. There was a loud crack—wood or bone, Maddock couldn't say—and the man rocked back. Not letting him get his feet under him, Maddock turned the *King Kooker*, connecting the hard edge with killer's other knee, hobbling him worse.

But the man refused to go down.

Okay then...

Aiming high again, Maddock jabbed with the oar, but two thick hands shot up to block the incoming blow to the face. Countering, Maddock aimed six inches lower and shoved the handle knob into the man's throat.

It was a solid hit, and the would-be killer dropped to his knees, wheezing for air. Maddock could have easily broken the man's windpipe with a harder blow, but he needed to keep him alive. Dead men didn't answer any questions.

A noise drew Maddock's attention but he relaxed when he saw Bones come around the corner. Sighing at seeing his friend alive and well, Maddock took one long step closer to the gasping man and drove his right knee into his face. The attacker fell backward onto the ground in a bloodied mess.

Satisfied that they were in the clear, Maddock was about to ask Bones how he was, but before he could speak, he heard the low wail of sirens.

"Great…" Bones mumbled, looking toward the back of the store. "Fire escape?"

Maddock shook his head. They might be able to make it in time but he had a different idea.

"Stay put, we aren't the enemy here." He started in the direction of the storefront, hands raised, only then noticing the new addition to Bones' wardrobe. "Nice hat."

Bones glanced up and then snarled, ripping off the bloodied hat, tossing it aside. It landed on the unconscious hitman's face as they walked off. "Thanks for sending me to the *Aisle from Hell* by the way. Paul Bunyan almost took my head off a couple times."

Two uniformed men rushed in, weapons drawn, cutting off any reply from Maddock. He and Bones just calmly stood there and waited to be cuffed, but the two policemen completely bypassed them and went after their attackers instead.

"It's okay," the store clerk said, from behind them. "I phoned the police—told them what happan. You are fine." He bowed slightly. "Thank you for stopping them."

Bones' lifted one eyebrow high. "Stopped them from what?"

The employee motioned to the store. "From robbing me."

Bones looked at Maddock and shrugged. "Um, you're welcome."

"Sure," Maddock said, scratching his head, "anytime."

Two more policemen arrived, struggling to drag the deadweight of *Machete Man* outside. Keeping up the fiction of being heroic bystanders, Maddock and Bones lent a hand.

After getting handshakes from the deputies, they headed back inside where they were met by a single, more intimidating officer. He just stood off to the side, jotting down notes on a small pad of paper. They had caused a good deal of damage and left two men bloodied and beaten. There were consequences even if the response had been justified.

The barrel-chested man walked over to them, a stern look on his face. He observed the two of them for a moment before speaking, studying them. "American?"

Maddock and Bones answered simultaneously.

"Yes."

"The real deal."

The officer looked at Bones. "What does that mean?"

"Cherokee," Bones replied, "you know Geronimo, peace pipes, and war paint."

The policeman turned to Maddock. "Asshole?"

Maddock burst out laughing and handed the cop his fake ID, confirming his nationality was indeed American. Even Bones grinned at the man's sense of humor and did the same. Looking them over for a second, the officer returned them and shook their hands.

"Thank you for your timely intervention, Mr. Jagger and Mr. Richardson. Henrik's mother..." he motioned to the store clerk, "She will be pleased to know he is fine."

"You know his mother?" Bones asked.

"I know everyone in Vikersund, but yes, I do. She is my wife."

Maddock smiled. "Henrik's your son then."

"Yes, he is. If there is anything I can do to thank you, please, let me know."

Maddock looked at Bones and then back to the officer. "Well…There is one thing."

Bones finished. "We're looking for a man named Torbjorn Sorensen. You wouldn't happen to know where he is, would you?"

FIVE

The third man—the stranger, known only as *Hoor*—shrunk into the narrow alley behind the store, distancing himself further from the failed attempt on the Americans' lives.

His name, Hoor, came from Norse mythology. He had been one of Odin's sons, and had killed his brother *Baldr* with their father's spear—Gungnir.

No one, not even his current employer knew his real identity. Hoor made sure that any trace to his past life had been erased. Documents were burned, so was his home. Even a few people along the way were eliminated.

He owed his training to those in the German Army and to a retired *Spetsnaz*—a Russian Special Forces soldier—one of the most ruthless military divisions in the world. Hoor's military career had been distinguished until one day when he had gotten a little too rough during an interrogation. The interviewee was a suspected arms dealer. Hoor had broken the man's wrists.

The prisoner—a Saudi national—was traded for additional intel and vowed revenge on Hoor soon after his release. Eventually, he held true to his promise and returned, approaching Hoor on the street. Words were shared and shots fired. Three civilians were killed in the altercation. Needing someone to blame, his bosses suspended Hoor for inciting a known terrorist and *retired* him from active duty. They agreed to let him off easy due to his stellar career and buried his involvement. But the powers that be had had enough of his outbursts and cut him loose a few weeks later. Yes, he was a free man, but his life was ruined.

That's when he started working as a freelance *contractor*—a mercenary. For the last ten years, he'd been traveling between Europe, Scandinavia, and Russia as a gun for hire. Mercenary work was natural for him. It was good pay—cash, always cash. He lived where he needed, never settling down for too long. Motels became his place of residence and depending on the country, he would book it under a different alias. He had eight such identities as of now, being able to speak four languages.

Continuing down the alley, his throwaway phone buzzed. He quickly checked it.

The text read, *Report.*

He replied, *Fail.*

This was his first time dealing with ScanoGen, but the same could not be said for the two Americans. These newcomers were not just amateurs. Their cunning display in the sporting goods store gave testament to that.

After a second, the phone vibrated again and read, *Continue.*

Right away.

The conversations with his employer were always like that. He'd been a few hours south of the border when he'd received a message about the job and jumped at the chance when he's read the email describing what he was going after.

There was only one Norse weapon that could do what Sorensen's email described.

Gungnir… I know it!

Hoor was fanatical about anything to do with the old gods. He truly believed in the mythology surrounding Odin, Frigg, Thor, Loki, and even his namesake, Hoor. It was in his veins. His family believed themselves to be of an ancient Germanic bloodline, one that worshipped the old ways centuries ago.

"Gungnir," he whispered to himself, squeezing the phone harder. He remembered seeing the latest Captain America movie, the hero crushing a soldier's radio with just his bare hands. He desperately wished he had the power to do the same now. He was a lean man, almost scrawny. He wanted to be more than what he was.

Maybe with Odin's spear, he would.

If Gungnir was somewhere in the forests to the north, it would be his, not ScanoGen's. He would use it and become something he dreamt about since birth.

Hoor would be the god he was meant to be.

But first, he needed to find Torbjorn Sorensen and dispose of the pesky American agents.

Hoor also needed to be careful as well. Another ScanoGen hire was supposedly close by, waiting for a call to extract him and the weapon. Where, or who, the other man was Hoor wasn't sure, and from what he could gather, if he should fail in his duty, the second contractor had orders to take him out and finish the mission himself.

Covering their asses, he thought. He sneered at the thought of losing his chance. *I will not fail.*

Maddock and Bones followed Henrik's father, the Chief of Police, who was also named Henrik. The senior Henrik Haugen led them away from town and into the forest.

"Tor and I used to come up here together in our younger days. We grew up together. He became a teacher and I went into law enforcement."

"Not to be ungrateful or anything," Bones said, "but

your English is spot on."

The gray-haired, bearded man nodded. "I was schooled just across the sea in England and learning your language was necessary. Students from all over the world studied there and English was obviously the most common tongue." He chuckled. "I was hopeless for my first term."

"So, you went to England to study law but ended up back in Vikersund?"

Chief Haugen glanced at Bones. "I didn't mean to stay. I came back after I graduated and found out that the former chief had passed away. The mayor asked me to take up the badge. He wanted someone younger, with personal knowledge of the town. Since I had family here, I agreed. Twenty-five years later and I'm still in Vikersund."

"And now with a wife and son," Maddock added.

"The mayor's daughter," he said, grinning.

"You old dog," Bones said, laughing aloud.

Haugen stopped them with a silent hand. The former SEALs understood the gestured and instantly paused. Maddock was tempted to draw his gun but he and Bones had already introduced themselves as reporters and not former military men with a knack for finding lost treasure.

"Anything in these woods we should worry about?" Maddock asked, searching the dark spaces between the boughs.

Haugen turned, eyeing the Americans hard. "You know, you two don't act like reporters." Maddock and Bones glanced at one another. "The way you took down those thugs in my son's store...If I had to guess, you both were in the military in the past."

Maddock decided to run with it. "In the past. We were both in the Navy together."

"And now?" Haugen asked eyebrow raised, trying to get more information out of them.

"Just reporters," Maddock quickly replied.

"Too bad," Haugen said, pulling out his pistol. He turned back to the woods. "Could've used an extra set of hands out here."

"Why's that?" Maddock asked.

"The wolves have been more active lately. Something has spooked them. And…" He trailed off.

"And?" Bones prompted.

"One of my deputies spoke to a local backwoodsman who says he saw a demon roaming the forest."

"A demon?" Bones fingered the blade of the hatchet hanging at his hip, one of the pair he'd wielded against the man in the store. Once Haugen agreed to help them find Sorensen, Henrik Jr. had given them their choice of equipment for the sojourn into the forest. before they headed out. Maddock had helped himself to a brand-new splitting axe, which he now carried slung across his back. Gripping his *weapons* again, Bones grinned. He preferred the double barrel approach and these hand axes seemed blessed with good luck.

"Yes, a demon," Haugen replied. "The forests of Vikersund have been long-rumored to be cursed— haunted. Of course, there has never been any evidence to support the claims."

"Ghost stories," Bones said, nodding. "We all have our ghosts…" He thought back to the terrifying ones from his childhood. All Native American cultures had them, the Cherokee people were no different.

"Any chance the demon showed up around the same

time Sorensen went missing?" Maddock asked.

Haugen again stopped, turning around. "Yes…it did." The look in his eyes was dead serious. Whatever happened to Sorensen, Haugen agreed that the recent sightings were somehow related.

"What's your interest in all this, Mr. Jagger? Don't tell me you're just here for a story about a champion small town axe thrower."

Maddock shrugged. "A champion small-town axe thrower isn't much of a story, but throw in a mysterious disappearance, and it goes prime time."

After a moment of thoughtful contemplation, Haugen sighed. "Tor made a discovery out here, something that was supposed to change history itself."

"Really?" Maddock prompted. "That big?"

"You sure you're only reporters for ESPN?" Haugen asked.

"We can leave this off the record if you'd like."

"I would appreciate it," Haugen replied. "Tourism is important to this town. We can't risk the welfare of its people by scaring off their main source of income." He looked ahead. "As far as what Tor found… I'm not sure." He started off again, speaking as he did. Maddock and Bones followed. "But if I know these lands as well as I believe I do, then we may be shown regardless of if we want to or not."

SIX

They made camp at nightfall, setting up in a three-person cold weather tent—also courtesy of Henrik jr.—in a small clearing. Haugen said the forecast called for little, to no, snow which was a relief for everyone. The tent's confines were tight, and unfortunately for Maddock, he was the smallest of the three men making a normally cramped experience even more so.

But at least the landscape outside was calm and beautiful. Tall, snow-covered trees surrounded them, swaying in a gentle, crisp mountain breeze. He understood why some people preferred the mountains to the beaches. He just wasn't one of them.

"Well," Bones said, trying to wriggle free of his partner's limbs, "at least we won't be cold tonight."

"Body heat is effective, yes," Haugen agreed, "but I would typically suggest snuggling with a pretty blonde over the likes of you."

Maddock grinned and Bones gave a snort of laughter. "I don't care what they say about you, Henrik. You're all right."

Maddock silently agreed. Haugen was a professional, not some bumbling small-town Barney Fife, but he also knew when to relax and act like a human. Maddock's impression of him improved even more when he passed around a flask.

"This is a local brew from a woodsman with no name," Haugen explained.

"Huh?" Bones replied, taking a tentative sniff. He'd been a heavy drinker in his younger years and now rarely drank hard liquor. He tilted it back quickly, splashing a few drops into his mouth A moment later, he gave a hoarse cough.

Haugen smiled wide. "Or maybe it's that we've never reported his name…"

"We should save that stuff in case the lantern runs out of white gas," Bones said blinking back tears. He passed the flask to Maddock, who took a similarly cautious sip and immediately agreed with Bones' assessment. Back in the Keys, he normally limited his own consumption to a couple bottles *Dos Equis* under a beautiful Florida sunset. Drinking moonshine in a tent in the Norwegian forest wasn't even a bucket list item.

A sound—not quite a howl, but more than a growl—reverberated in the air around them. Bones, instantly cold stone sober, sat up and whipped out one of his axes. Maddock gripped his larger variant, wishing he could draw his sidearm instead. He had a feeling they'd soon have to break their cover and use their guns.

Surprising both men, Haugen went for his own pistol. Whatever was out there, apparently wasn't the norm. If Haugen was spooked…

The close confines of the tent suddenly seemed a lot closer and a lot more confining.

"Wolf?" Maddock asked, hoping it was. But he thought back to their briefing with Tam. There was one word that stuck out more than the rest… Creature.

"If it is, it's like no wolf I've ever heard before."

Dammit, Maddock thought.

"The ghost stories," Bones said, "what exactly did the people see?"

Dowsing their interior light off, Haugen answered in a whisper barely loud enough for them to hear. "There were three separate accounts of a large beast of some kind. No one got close enough to get a better look, however, so there are some inconsistencies."

"Who could blame them," Bones remarked, gripping his axe tighter. "My sphincter is puckered just hearing about it. I doubt the best laxative in the world would do jack right now."

Maddock rolled his eyes in the dark.

Haugen went on. "The one thing that was dead on with each account was a low howl—"

"Like the one we just heard," Maddock finished, breathing in deep. He needed to make a verdict soon. Looking at Haugen's shadowy form, he quietly decided that they could trust him with the truth. He reached around the small of his back and gripped his pistol. Bullets were *always* better than blades. No one ever regretted bringing a gun to a knife fight. It was always— *always*—the other way around.

If it came to it, they'd act with full force. Tam understood that they might have to go Rambo on people from time to time to get the job done. It was a risk they were all willing to take, a necessary one.

But not yet, he thought, hoping that whatever was out there would pass them by, leaving their ruse intact for a little while longer.

The low, guttural growl echoed around them again, only this time, it was followed by another, more familiar howl. And then another...and another... A pack of wolves was nearby which was *never* a good thing. Whatever was out there, it seemed to be getting the attention of one of the region's apex predators.

"Sounds like three or four," Haugen whispered. "Not good…"

"Which part?" Bones asked. "The wolves, or the

number of wolves?"

"Both," Haugen replied. "There should be more."

"More?" Maddock asked, staying calm.

"If it's the pack I'm thinking of, yes. There should be eight of them in total. We should be hearing a chorus of howls right now. They are very vocal and easy to locate usually. It also makes them easy to avoid."

"Avoid… Right." Bones gave a harsh laugh.

"So," Maddock said, "whatever is out there is after the wolves."

"Sounds like it," Haugen replied. "And—"

A sharp cry cut him off and he cursed under his breath.

"There goes another one," Bones mumbled.

"*Faen*," Haugen grumbled.

Maddock was about to ask what it meant but decided it wasn't the time. Either way, Haugen's rigid body language seemed to confirm that it wasn't a pleasant word to use, which meant it would probably soon find its way into Bones' vocabulary.

A soft pattering of footfalls followed the last cries they'd heard. "The wolves," Haugen said. "They're coming this way." He slowly and with great care, unzipped the panel over the screen window.

Two of them *yipped* at one another as they passed just as a third slower—possibly injured—one sauntered by. It trailed its kin by a good twenty feet. They could just see the animal's outlines thanks to the bright, overhead moonlight.

As the third wolf continued past them, they heard it whimpering in pain. It was definitely hurt.

But by what? Maddock asked himself.

Whatever it was, it decided that bulldozing through

the tent was easier than skittering around it. The nylon shock-poles popped loose with the impact and the tent collapsed. As the wolf's cold paws pressed down on them, the three men wrestled out from under it, thrashing and bumping into each other. Knees hit faces and elbows hit everything else. Finally, they stopped, entangled in one another, like a chaotic string of Christmas lights.

"Careful with that axe, Eugene," Bones muttered as he pulled his left hand from between Maddock's thighs. Maddock squirmed to extricate his legs free beneath Haugen's back, and the police chief had to practically lift himself off the ground to get free of both Americans.

"Ouch," Maddock said, wincing from a shot to his more *sensitive* area.

A yelp turned into a cry of terror and then silence. All three men froze. The had come from right outside their upside-down tent flap. Maddock knew they had two choices. Freeze in place and hope for the best, or run like hell and hope for the best. Judging by the fate of the wolves, at least one of those choices was a death sentence.

By mutual unspoken accord, they chose the former, remaining absolutely still, not even daring to breathe. The only noise around them was the ripping and tearing of flesh. The wolf had become a meal for something far fiercer than it. The tent was between them and the creature, but they could hear everything—the wet tearing and the crack of bones breaking. After a few moments of indulgence, the beast sniffed loudly. Its inhalations were like that of a hound, fluttering in quick successions.

It found another scent, Maddock thought. He tapped Bones' leg, getting his partner's attention without having to speak. Hopefully, Bones would understand what he wanted.

Without pause, Maddock drew his pistol, and as silently as he could. Bones quietly did the same, getting a look from Haugen. In the dim light, Bones shrugged and put a finger to his lips. They would happily explain later... *If* they made it out alive.

A large shadow looming over their tent, blotting out the moonlight entirely. It was absolutely massive but impossible to see exactly how big without leaving the *safety* of their man-sized ravioli. Maddock hoped the fresh blood would mask their own scent, making the beast think the tent, and therefore its occupants, inedible. But once a single razor-sharp claw poked through and began tearing at the fabric, he knew they were screwed.

Leveling his pistol at the slowly increasing slit, he gently squeezed the trigger. He was *this* close to firing but stopped when he heard their salvation charging out of the woods behind them. Wolves, at least three of them, pounded through the snow and leaped at the creature, trampling the trapped men as they did. As the behemoth was knocked back, it gripped the tent fabric, shredding it as it fell back, exposing the men inside to the elements... And to the carnage surrounding them.

Fur and blood went flying, as did two of the wolves. One got up and snarled, leaping back into motion, the other one didn't. It was horribly bent around the base of a nearby tree. The crack of its spine sent a shiver through Maddock's body. Then something tugged at the fabric, and like a peeled banana, the cold-weather tent fell away from them completely.

They were right smack in the middle of the rage-filled brawl.

Maddock dove into Haugen, barely avoiding another airborne wolf, just as Bones rolled the other way, but he wasn't avoiding one of Mother Nature's creatures... He was avoiding something from the depths of Hell itself.

"Holy *faen*" he whispered.

It stood nearly eight feet tall and was covered in thick, matted fur. It was built like a human... but not. Its arms were longer and thicker than a man's, almost resembling those of an ape, but it was not a primate either. The only parts that weren't covered in an animal's coat, were its thighs and feet, upper arms and hands, and... its face.

His face.

"Torbjorn?" Haugen asked upon seeing his friend's still human features.

In the moonlight, Maddock saw it too. The face looked exactly like the picture of Torbjorn Sorensen in Tam's file, except for the elongated jaw, fangs, and dark angry eyes.

No... "angry" wasn't the right word.

They burned with fury.

For a split second, the *TorBeast's* face softened. Then, he blinked and sneered. Something inside the man-thing's mind had snapped, turning Sorensen into an uncontrollable rage-monster.

But for a moment, Haugen *had* broken through. Was it possible to bring this man back from the rage-filled void?

There was no chance to even attempt it. The two remaining wolves leaped into action again. One of them latched onto Sorensen's wrist, while the other turned on Bones.

Without giving it a chance, he put three rounds in its chest, cringing as he did. It wasn't the animal's fault. It was just doing what instinct had programmed it to do.

Kill or be killed.

The gunshots reverberated around them, making the last wolf let go. But instead of re-engaging its foe, it turned and fled deeper into the trees. Now, Maddock, Bones, and Chief Haugen were alone with Sorensen.

Maddock didn't know if that was a good thing or a bad thing. If Sorensen still retained any of his humanity, he'd be able to think like a man but fight like an eight-foot-tall Yeti on steroids. But they might also be able to reach the man inside the beast's skin.

After watching the wolf dart away, Sorensen turned and faced them. As he did, three pistols leveled on his chest, but Haugen spoke to him in their shared tongue. Each word came out slow and deliberate, like talking to an infant.

Sorensen advanced a step but stopped when Haugen yelled, "*Stoppe!*"

He continued speaking in firm voice getting what seemed to be a hint of understanding. Raising his gun barrel higher, in line with his friend's face, Haugen said one more thing.

"*Ga.*"

Maddock and Bones were about to pull their respective triggers, but Sorensen wheeled around and took off running into the dark. Haugen was in motion as well, moving to their ruined tent. He grabbed his pack and slung it over his shoulder.

"What are you doing?" Maddock asked.

"We can track him and try to figure out what happened," Haugen yelled, starting off in the direction

Sorensen had gone.

"What do you mean 'what happened'?" Bones asked, trotting to catch up to the police chief.

"I…have…a theory," Haugen replied, panting heavily while he spoke. "But…it would require you…to believe in the unbelievable."

"Done," Bones said quickly. He and Maddock had seen enough weirdness to know better than to dismiss even the craziest story out of hand. This would be no different.

"What do you gentlemen know about berserkers?"

After their airborne conversation with Tam, both men knew a decent amount about them, but from the look on Haugen's face, Maddock suspected they were about to hear a side of the story that wasn't covered on a Wikipedia page.

SEVEN

Hoor watched in shock as the beast cut down the wolves with ease, a feat that should've been impossible for any man to accomplish. He smiled.

But you aren't a man, are you?

The sight of the berserker was something Hoor had longed to witness since he was a child.

Over a hundred years ago, locals swore they heard a battle raging throughout the forest, like the trees themselves were crying out in pain. Hate-filled roars echoed down the mountainside, giving the proposed cursed lands an even deeper connotation.

He had to have found Gungnir, Hoor thought, grinning ear to ear. His body shook with terror but also with anticipation. He was as scared as the other men to be sure. But where they sought to help the creature—Sorensen—Hoor sought to become him.

Dressed head to toe in all-white snow gear, Hoor continued following close behind the local and the two Americans. He would let them find what they needed and quickly move in for the kill and take it. ScanoGen was expecting a progress report in the next few hours and Hoor hoped to be off the grid by then.

With my prize.

The real secret of becoming a berserker wasn't only the physical transformation. The important thing was controlling the newfound gifts. Those who could were all but immortal. They felt no pain in battle and gained a superhuman, godlike, physical strength. That was why his employer wanted it. They didn't care about the spear; they just wanted to find the biological mechanism underlying its transformation effect in order to produce a serum capable of turning men into monsters.

But Hoor wanted Gungnir itself. A berserker that could also wield Odin's chosen weapon could lead, and then, control an army of berserkers. He'd be able to change others and become their master.

Feeling his chest, Hoor fingered what lay inside his coat's pocket. It was a small book, depicting the valknut and Gungnir together. His family belonged to an ancient sect of believers whose sole purpose was to obtain and wield Gungnir. But unlike the other members, Hoor's lineage believed themselves to be direct descendants of King Harald Fairhair. It gave them the birthright to wield Gungnir. Sorensen probably hadn't been aware of it, but his own great-grandfather, Johan Larsen, belonged to the organization as well.

Unless he found Larsen's journal....

Every member kept one, chronicling what they discovered about the subject. Each year, they'd meet and exchange notes. But as time waned, and members died off, the fellowship disbanded. World War II was particularly harmful as most of the sect lived in Europe and fought for the armies of one side or the other. Some of the survivors still continued the search, but most fell into obscurity like the Larsen clan. When Johan disappeared, their line's search stalled.

Until now, of course.

Hoor remembered his own grandfather talking about the *Children of Odin* and their purpose in the world. They were meant to rule it, and with how most upper-class offspring saw their family's wealth, the group's descendants believed Gungnir was theirs by birthright. It wasn't until Hoor began getting bullied in school repeatedly that he bought into the ramblings of the crazed old man.

Hoor's father died when he was young, leaving him at the mercy of his mentally unbalanced *farfar*. His grandfather's rants about the old ways, and the gods they praised, were well known in their hometown, but little could be done to squelch his behavior since he wasn't at all violent. Theo was a courteous man in public, but in private, he was something else entirely.

He never once raised a hand to his grandson, but what Hoor witnessed was some of the most demented things he'd ever seen. Theo worshipped Odin as a Satanist would the devil. His rituals called for sacrifices of all kinds. He said the gods would look down on them with pride if they did what they did.

Hoor participated after he lost a tooth to a classmate's fist. Theo guaranteed it would give him the strength to defeat his enemies. What it really did was give him the confidence in his own growing psychosis. That was when Julian Solheim became Hoor, son of Odin.

Something in his mind had broken. It eventually mended with the calling of becoming a god at its forefront. He lived and breathed the mythology his family alleged.

Ten years later, Hoor sought out the grade school bully, killing him in an alleyway with his bare hands. He still remembered the feeling of the man's life ending while Hoor's hands gripped his neck. He would kill these men just as easily, except, with something a little more damaging. Gripping the lightweight submachine gun, he smiled.

And if the firepower couldn't stop them, he knew

something else that would. He would use the might of Gungnir and eviscerate his prey. Then, he'd drink their blood as a reward for his victory.

Theo will be honored.

"**Who are you**, really?" Haugen asked, impressed with the larger man's tracking abilities. The Cherokee would stop every so often and study the ground in front of them, mumbling to himself the entire time. Haugen could've done the same, the tracks were immense, but watching the man who called himself Keith Richardson do it was like a work of art being completed right before him.

"Forgive me, Chief Haugen," Maddock replied, "but I can't tell you our real names. What I can tell you is that we are here on behalf of our government. And we were both in the Navy together. That was the truth."

"Please, just Henrik," he said, snuffing out the formalities. He again studied them. "SEALs?"

Neither man responded which gave Haugen the answer he sought. Yes, they were. "Good then," he said.

"Good?" Bones asked, kneeling in the snow.

"Yes, it means you are very capable in a fight—a capability we will most likely need in the night ahead."

Maddock smiled. "We've been in a scrap or two, yes."

"Why are you here?"

Maddock glanced at him. "All I can say is that a third-party is involved, and if we don't get there first, the danger won't be contained in this forest."

"The men at my son's store," Haugen said, getting an epiphany, "they were there for you, weren't they?"

Bones stood and stretched his back. "Yeah...sorry about that, Henrik. For what it's worth, we don't know who they were and we certainly didn't expect to be attacked right then and there."

"Hired goons," Maddock added. "Their employer was being cautious and wanted someone on hand to collect what awaits."

"Odin's berserkers," Haugen's eyes widened a bit. "Someone wants the ability to make other men into berserkers like Torbjorn. An army with the abilities would be unstoppable."

"And uncontrollable," Maddock said, and then quickly added. "Of course, we don't know that for sure."

"It sure looked like it to me," Bones said, moving faster. "Come on, the trail goes straight through here."

The three men moved as one, guns at the ready. They'd been on the move for a couple of hours and thankfully the snow that Haugen said wouldn't be there wasn't. If it had been snowing, they would've lost the trail long ago. As long as the creature that used to be Torbjorn Sorensen didn't double back, or worse, climb a tree, they'd be able to track him down eventually.

The moonlight seemed brighter now, but he knew it was just that his eyes had adjusted to the darkness, having done plenty of night ops in the past.

"Any idea where we're headed?" Bones asked from the front of the group.

"Just deeper into the forest," Haugen replied, easily keeping pace. "The stories get stranger the further you get from civilization. Tales of the howling beasts become more frequent too. Our ancestors spoke of the evils of these woods centuries ago. But as technology arrived and information became widespread, people believed in the legends less and less, since there was no evidence to prove it."

"Yep," Bones said, "except for the flat earth morons and their crowd, people want hard data now. The belief in something that's deemed *odd* is looked at as stupid."

"Just like Nessie hunters," Maddock said, agreeing with his partner. "Many legitimate scientists have lost their careers over it. Credibility is everything in their world and cryptids were mostly seen as off limits—a fool's errand."

"But this is completely different," Haugen said. "The berserker warriors have been well documented in history. Of course, no one really knows the extent of the embellishments, but there is no question that they did exist."

"Embellishment like what we just saw?" Bones asked, wryly.

Haugen nodded. "You are very right but we don't yet know the whole story. Maybe there's a reason no one has found anything looking like what Torbjorn has become."

"Like what?" Maddock asked, interested in the theory.

"Berserkers were said to go on a bloodthirsty rampage in battle. Their minds were lost, giving them an inner strength no man could best. Some even believe that it only occurs when they're threatened or in conflict—like in battle, for instance."

"So," Bones said, "it only happens during a fight."

"Like the stories of a parent lifting a car off their kid," Maddock said. "A switch gets thrown during moments of severe stress that causes the human brain and body to work together differently. It's why an ape is so much stronger than a human of the same size. Their bodies are hardwired differently. I'm not an expert on the subject, however. But to me, this sounds like an adrenaline spike or something."

"You're saying that Sorensen became that because of stress?" Bones asked, disbelieving. "In that case, I'm screwed." He looked up from the ground to his friend. "So are you."

Maddock shook his head. "No, whatever he found up here did it but maybe the threat of the wolves triggered something worse. Then, when he saw Henrik here, he fled. He seemed to recognize you."

"Yes," Haugen agreed, "and that's what frightens me the most."

"Why is that?" Bones asked.

"Because I'm not sure I can bring myself to kill Tor if the time comes. If the man I know is still in there, then there's a chance we can save him."

Maddock stopped, halting the others. "But..." he said, letting the word hang in the air, "If we can't and he threatens our lives, we *will* take him out."

Haugen's eyes glistened with emotion. "Let's hope it doesn't come to that."

As Maddock and Haugen continued to converse, Bones moved off a few more yards, further inspecting the way ahead. Something felt off and when he found another set of prints, he knew something was definitely wrong,

"Over here."

Maddock and Haugen hurried over, confused by what they saw. It was the trail, but a smaller footprint continued on after the larger ones. They were still bigger than the average man's, but nowhere near as big as the berserker's.

"It is him," Haugen said with hope in his voice. "Tor, he's becoming human again."

"They can do that?" Bones asked.

"I don't know, but if these tracks belong to the same body, then it means there's a chance that the beast is becoming my friend again."

"What of his mind?" Maddock asked, not letting Haugen continue too far down *that* path. Hope sometimes blinding to the truth. "Will he still be the same man as before."

"I can't answer that," Haugen admitted. He buried his eyes in Maddock. "If you've gone through what he has, would you still be the man you are now?"

The answer was an obvious one.

No, you wouldn't.

EIGHT

"Everybody quiet! Listen." Bones' voice was as hushed as ever. Something was off in the distance, moaning. It almost sounded like a deep whimper, like someone, or some*thing*, was crying.

As the tracks continued to shrink, they became harder and harder to follow. A light dusting began as they moved higher up the mountain too, obscuring the now, man-sized footprints. But instead of relying on only a visual trail, they also had an audible one too.

It had been hours since they started off to the north and Bones had yet to move them off course. Sorensen was headed for something out in the middle of nowhere and Haugen knew it could only be the place where it had all begun. The tomb must've been just ahead.

"When we get where we're going," Maddock instructed, "Stay back and let us clear the area first." Haugen went to argue but Maddock stopped him. "I know you're used to being in charge, but trust us on this, we know what we're doing."

Swallowing his pride, Haugen simply nodded and let the two Americans lead the way, watching their backs instead. There were still other predators out there besides Torbjorn Sorensen.

He still couldn't believe it. The always gentle giant of a man was now a monster from antiquity. What was even scarier than that was there existed something tangible in the world that could cause it. Haugen had seen plenty of science fiction movies over the years and even had the time to sit down and read a couple of books in the genre, but living it was something else entirely.

The Americans were nice enough and treated him with a great deal of respect. It's another way he knew them to be former soldiers. There was respect between military folk and local law enforcement.

Well, most of the time anyway.

He thought back a few months to a brash, loud-mouthed American tourist he had the displeasure of dealing with before. Like the two men before him, he was clearly military at one point. The visitor's name didn't ring any bells, but what he remembered most about him was his foul mouth and obnoxious sense of humor. He claimed to be "passing through" and instead decided to stay a week. It wasn't even that he was trying to rub anyone the wrong way either, it was just the man's natural personality. The quiet people of Vikersund couldn't wait for him to leave. How that pretty, tattooed Frenchwoman put up with such a character he couldn't fathom.

"Kane…" he mumbled to himself, "that was his name."

"There's a clearing up ahead," Bones said, motioning them forward. "And a body."

Guns up, the Americans cleared a small opening in the forest, giving the space a thorough 360-degree sweep. But it was easy to see that there was nothing there.

Seeing what was obviously a dead wolf, Bones put his hands on his hips, perplexed. "Huh."

"What?" Haugen asked, carefully inspected the body.

"The tracks are gone." He looked up. "The snowfall covered them."

"We lost him?" Haugen asked, looking up.

"He didn't say that," Maddock replied, looking at

Bones, "did you?"

Bones turned and grinned. "The big oaf couldn't have just vanished." He glanced at Haugen. "No offense... But these trees and bushes also look undisturbed."

"So, where'd he go?" Haugen asked.

What would I do... Maddock thought, his shoulders perking up some. "Camouflage. He hid his path."

Quickly, the three men split up and began yanking away and pushing aside every piece of growth they could reach. If necessary, they'd climb the trees and spider monkey around. Just as Maddock was about to, a section off to his right was cleared. He raised his pistol at the sight. An opening just large enough for a grown man to fit through was there and beyond it laid only darkness.

"The moonlight barely reaches," Haugen said, peeking in.

Maddock clicked on a small flashlight and pointed it up through the opening, finding only tree branches. "Wouldn't be able to see it from the air either. The problem with that is—"

"Trees don't grow this way without help," Bones finished, pointing his own flashlight to the ground. He bent over and took a closer look at the path ahead. "Man-made... Well, I think it's safe to say we found our tomb entrance."

"But who made it?"

"That, my friends," a voice said from behind, "is something I'd also like to know."

They turned but before they could lift their weapons to fire, a line of bullets tore into the ground just inches in front of their toes. Maddock and Bones both dove to the ground, rolling to make themselves less of a target, aiming their pistols in the direction from which the assault had come.

"Don't!" The shooter shouted, from behind a large tree trunk. The only thing visible was his weapon and face, an impossible shot to take. "I will kill you and take what's mine," they paused their counter assault, "or you can help me retrieve it—"

"And then you'll kill us anyway," Bones finished. "We know the drill, buddy. Why should we, huh?"

The newcomer poked his head and rifle out further. Maddock recognized him immediately as the dark-haired stranger. Grinning, his aim shifted to Haugen. He stood alone, dead center in the clearing. "I'll shoot your friend. He's innocent in all this, yes? Do you need his death on your conscience?"

Grumbling an incoherent response, Bones' shoulders sagged a little. Maddock's, on the other hand, didn't. "I saw you in town before we were attacked. Who are you?"

The man smiled. "I am Hoor."

"You're a what now?" Bones asked.

"Hoor," Haugen said. "He was one of Odin's sons."

"Oh," Bones said, "a fanatic nutjob, are we?"

Hoor's icy blue eyes, squinted, angered. "Shall I kill you instead?" His aim switched from Haugen to Bones.

Maddock and Bones would much rather have the guns on them instead of a local. If they died, so be it, but no one else needed to. Plus, Haugen was armed still. Hoor had yet to tell them to drop their weapons.

And I think I know why, Maddock thought, speaking quickly. "I'll make you a deal."

Hoor's eyebrows raised. "A deal?"

"Yes," Maddock said, holstering his gun, stepping forward and in front of Haugen. "If you agree to let us go, we'll retrieve what you're looking for."

"And what do I seek?" Hoor asked, wanting to see what they knew.

"The origin of the berserker virus."

Hoor's eyes opened. "Virus?"

Maddock shrugged. "What else could it be? Since you followed us here, I'm assuming you saw what killed those wolves earlier."

Hoor nodded. "I did. It was fabulous."

"Fabulous? That is what you call it?" Haugen asked, shocked at the gunman's use of the word. "It was evil—nothing more."

The ghost of a smile played across his face. "I know."

Maddock and Bones looked at each other. For a hired ScanoGen goon, this guy came across as more of an obsessive psychopath than a simple mercenary.

Bones voiced as much. "You're going to screw over your employer, aren't you? You're here for yourself."

"Not as stupid as you look. I've been searching for clues to this place for a long time, collecting as much information on it as possible. I built a name for myself and stayed in the area with the hopes of eventually being called to it. It just so happens that I was contracted to retrieve exactly that earlier this week."

"You're here for Gungnir," Maddock said.

The only reply he received was a sadistic leer.

The soft moaning they had heard earlier picked up again, coming from somewhere within the manmade pathway. There was no doubt what it was now. Sorensen was sobbing.

Who can blame the guy? Bones thought. "So," he said, "all you want is the freaking spear and then you'll leave?"

"Yes," Hoor replied, "you have my word. I won't harm any of you." He fought to hide another smile.

"Fine," Maddock said, moving to the opening, "we'll do it. All of us." The last part was to ensure that Haugen would be along with them. If he could appeal to Sorensen's human side, maybe, just maybe, they could sway him to help.

With one arm, Maddock coaxed Haugen through the opening in the shrubbery, never once taking his eyes off Hoor. Bones was next and then Maddock himself. He continued backward until they were all out of sight.

Turning, he found Bones and Haugen staring at the ground in front of them. Stepping around the two men, Maddock saw what stalled their retreat.

Blood... A lot of it. A trail of the stuff coated the stone path as far as they could see.

Another wolf?

"Come on," Maddock said, setting their pace. The three men took off together in a controlled jog, putting as much distance between them and the gun-toting lunatic as they could. They kept their footfalls as quiet as possible and headed straight for the tomb, careful not to slip in the slick layer of crimson.

A few moments later, they stopped and stared again—but not at another kill.

The outside of the tomb was unremarkable in construction but Maddock knew that most crypts hid their valuables within. The outside being bland was actually the best defense against looters. An ordinary structure gave off the same sense of what laid inside. A gorgeous monument almost always guaranteed that riches were hidden within.

Ordinary would be nice, Maddock thought. *Please, be*

ordinary.

But as they crossed the threshold, Maddock knew it was going to be anything but *normal*. They were about to explore an ancient tomb, which probably hid a virus that could make someone go *berserk*, not to mention a creature that had just obliterated an entire pack of wolves without so much as breaking a sweat.

All right, let's get this done.

Hoor didn't trust the Americans, and as soon as they disappeared from sight, he quietly pursued them. He went to enter the stone path but was stopped by something buzzing in his pocket. The high-tech GPS unit was sent along with his instructions and would track his exact location within a few yards of where he stood. Conveniently, it also doubled as a communication device which was extremely helpful when out in the wilderness.

Looking down at the screen, he sneered when he read the message.

Failure to report. Specialists inbound. ETA 30 minutes.

Cursing himself, Hoor knew he'd taken too long to track the men. But he had no choice. If he'd gone ahead of them and run into the berserker or even the wolves, he'd already be dead. Even with ScanoGen not knowing his own personal goals, there was no way of acquiring his prize before they arrived. Rushing into a tomb populated by a police officer, two former soldiers, and a monster, wasn't the smartest thing to do.

Hopefully, they'll kill each other and I can walk in and take it.

He started a timer on his watch and set it to twenty-five minutes. He needed to be gone by then. If not, he'd have to figure out a way to ditch the incoming six-man team and make off with the spear.

He looked up from his watch and visualized the tomb, smiling as he did. Maybe there was another way to rid him of everyone. He could just sit by and wait for the *specialists* to arrive. They'd go in guns blazing and kill everyone, except maybe the beast. Hoor knew *it* wouldn't die so easily. He recalled an excerpt describing the berserkers from memory. It was written almost 800 years ago by an Icelandic historian named, Snorri Sturluson.

"His men rushed forward without armor, were as mad as dogs or wolves, bit their shields, and were strong as bears or wild oxen, and killed people at a blow, but neither fire nor iron told upon them. This was called Berserkergang."

Hoor wanted to be one of them. He needed to be one of them. It was his calling—his destiny. The meek boy, Julian, would finally become a god in the flesh. Then, he would create an army of his own and set out into the world around him.

NINE

The three men covered their flashlights so that only the smallest amount illuminated the entrance tunnel. Haugen was awed at the beauty in the otherwise simple construction. The walls, incredibly smooth, rose eight feet, ending in a perfectly cut arch above their heads. It was like they were walking through the ancient corridors of a centuries-old castle, not a hidden mountain tomb.

The whimpering increased in volume with every step they took, reminding Maddock of a wounded animal as it cowered in death. He seriously doubted Sorensen was dying, he didn't even think the man had been injured in his fight with the wolf pack. No, the changed man was scared and terrified of what he'd become.

"Look," Bones whispered, tipping his chin to the right-hand wall.

Maddock noticed five grooves cut into it, running as far as his muted light could reach. Holding his hand out, he inserted his fingers into each of the grooves and found that they barely fit—they were close, though. Sorensen had definitely shrunk down in size, but Maddock also remembered the man's profile. He was six-seven, taller than Bones and over half a foot taller than Maddock. Naturally, his hands would be bigger.

Bones mimicked Maddock and found that his own fingers fit into the grooves better. His larger hand proved Maddock's theory correct. Sorensen was indeed back down to his human size. But from the evidence in front of them, he still sported a set of killer claws. Apparently, not everything returned to normal after he came down off his *anger high.*

More bellowing cries froze them in place, earning an uncomfortable grumble from Haugen. He was becoming impatient but had yet to challenge Maddock's instructions or tactics. They were going to take it slow and steady and hope not to get themselves killed. Haugen, conversely, wanted to rush right into his *friend's* open maw and then check things out after the fact.

Bones stepped in before it happened. "Careful… I'm not sure he's your friend anymore."

Haugen clearly disagreed but didn't question the assessment. Even if Sorensen could be helped, there was still the matter of what to do with Gungnir. There was also the weirdo outside waiting for them.

"We need to find a back door out of here when we get the chance," Maddock said, getting a nod of agreement from Bones.

"Yup, I have no intention of ever seeing that creep again."

"Nor I," Haugen added, checking behind them as he spoke. "His mind is warped beyond repair." Seeing nothing, he turned and continued forward, squeezing the handle of his service pistol as hard as he could. He needed to release his rising anxiety…

"I think it opens up ahead," Maddock said, grinding to a halt. They carefully listened to the world around them, but only heard the same sorrowful moans.

One by one, they exited the tunnel and stepped into a naturally formed cave. The rock formations, however, weren't what held their attention. What did was the remains of a second wolf, and huddled in front of an open coffin, its killer.

Sorensen.

The man was still covered in animal fur, head in his

hands, wailing loudly, tears streaming from the corners of his eyes. He was so lost in his torment that he failed to notice them enter and slowly approach.

Haugen held up his hand, asking Maddock and Bones to stay back a bit. They obliged, knowing their leadership would only get them so far. The next phase of their mission was up to Haugen. Either they left the tomb alive or became permanent residents of it.

Alive works for me, Maddock thought, cringing as Haugen knelt only feet away from Sorensen. Then, in a soft voice, the brave police chief addressed his longtime friend.

"Tor…"

Sorensen quickly lifted his head and made eye contact with Haugen. They watched as the changed man's face went from one of fright to one of vague recollection. He was beginning to remember who the man kneeling in front of him was.

"Heh… Hen-rik?"

"Yes, Tor, it's me. I'm here, old friend."

Sorensen looked behind Haugen, to Maddock and then Bones. A growl, like that of a distressed dog, emanated from deep within the history teacher's throat. He wasn't pleased to see strangers.

Haugen squelched his fear. "They're friends, Tor. They're here with me. They helped me find you."

"F-find me?"

"Yes, you went missing a few days ago. No one has seen you since you found this place."

Speaking of which, how did he even send the email? Maddock wondered. *Another time for that….*

Haugen looked around but kept talking in calm, soothing tones. "I remembered where we used to camp and we searched for you. We almost gave up until you and the wolves showed up. We followed your tracks and…" He faltered. "And we want to help."

"You can't help!" Sorensen roared, standing tall. He was roughly the same height as Bones but looked like he outweighed the American by a good thirty pounds. In his full berserker form, Sorensen may have weighed another hundred more.

"Tell me what happened?" Haugen asked, standing as well. His eyes found something clutched against Sorensen's chest—a small book. He held onto it like an infant, firm, yet, impossibly gentle.

Haugen eyed the journal. This didn't go unnoticed.

Slowly, Sorensen held out the book, offering it to Haugen. Carefully, Haugen flipped open the cover and saw it was written entirely in strange symbols. "Runes," he murmured. "You can read them, can't you Tor?" He closed it and handed it back to Sorensen. As he did, Maddock saw the valknut and spear pressed into the cover.

"What does it say?" Haugen asked.

Sorensen grunted and turned away, stepping around the coffin and through a massive collection of gold and jewels. He stopped near the occupant's head, gripping the black stone's lip. Maddock and Bones cautiously advanced, staying a couple of feet behind. Both men still held their guns but had them hidden behind their backs just in case things went south.

"Fair… Hair…" Sorensen said.

Haugen looked at the corpse. "King Harald? This is Harald Fairhair?"

Sorensen grunted again and nodded.

"He find… He take…"

Haugen looked over his shoulder and explained. "Harald Fairhair was Norway's first king. He unified our land, and if I'm not mistaken…" he glanced at Sorensen who simply nodded. "He used berserkers in battle."

"*Ulfhednar*," Sorensen said.

Haugen translated. "It is what Odin was said to call his wolf-warriors—his berserkers. It's what Fairhair called them too."

All from Gungnir I bet, Maddock thought.

He and Bones quickly moved to the foot of the coffin and looked inside. Running almost the entire length of the crypt was a deadly looking black spear, carved with symbols that reminded him of Viking runes. But the construction was futuristic in design and definitely *way* ahead of its time.

"Aliens," Bones whispered to Maddock.

"What?" Maddock asked, not hearing him.

"Aliens. Chariots of the Gods. But no anal probes."

Maddock rolled his eyes. He didn't care where it came from at the moment. What mattered most was Sorensen and Hoor. But yes, if he had to guess, he would've agreed with his partner's initial hypothesis. It was undeniably not of this world.

"It… made from…" Sorensen searched for the right words, "Space metal."

Bones elbowed Maddock, silently mouthing the words, "Told you so."

Sorensen continued, struggling with every word. "I touch." Sadness once again crept onto his face. "I want. I have evil in heart."

"You wanted to take it," Haugen said, understanding. "A find like this would be one for the ages. The great king's grave and a legendary weapon of the gods." It was truly a history buff's dream scenario. But in this case, it ended up being Sorensen's nightmare.

"Tor," Haugen said, getting the man's attention. "What does the book say?"

"It… Journal. It… Warning… No touch. Curse. Anger. Hate." He closed his eyes. "Sorrow." He put a hand on his chest. "Me."

"You feel all of that?" Haugen asked, his eyes watering.

Sorensen nodded again. "Me. It also explain use."

"You mean directions on how to wield it," Maddock said.

"Touch to man's heart," Sorensen explained. "Touch it and control him forever."

Then, the big guy turned away and sauntered over to the rear of the cave. Instead of leaning against the wall like Maddock thought he would, Sorensen disappeared from sight, morphing into it.

"Um…" Bones mumbled. "Dude is David Copperfield all of a sudden? What gives?"

Maddock approached and found a secondary tunnel cut diagonally into the rear of the room. It acted as perfect camouflage if you didn't know what to look for. Stepping in and fully uncovering his flashlight for the first time, Maddock counted three other tunnels branching off from the one he now stood in. A small alcove was tucked around the corner and he found Sorensen quietly sitting by himself, whispering in a language he didn't understand.

Wanting nothing more than to give the man peace, Maddock backed away and re-entered the main chamber. Bones and Haugen were speaking softly to one another as he did.

"What do we do with him?" Bones asked.

"I honestly don't know," Haugen replied, scratching his bearded chin. "Either way, Hoor is still going to expect the spear as payment in return for our lives."

"He ain't letting us walk away that easy," Bones said.

"We can give him the slip," Maddock said, smiling. "There are other tunnels, branching off deeper into the mountain. One of them may even lead to an exit."

"But where?" Bones asked.

"Does it matter?"

Neither man could argue. Anything was better than the alternative. They needed to leave unnoticed, or at the very least, get Hoor lost in the corridors and then double back to the main chamber.

Maddock turned and faced the coffin, eyeing the spear...Gungnir. "What do we do with it?"

"We can't touch it, that's for sure," Bones said, laughing. "I've done a lot of questionable things in my life, but touching Obadiah's scepter won't be one of them."

"What was it that Sorensen said about touching it?" Maddock asked, ignoring Bones. "Something about his intentions."

"He said he had evil in his heart when he grabbed it," Haugen said. "Do you think it can sense the wielder's agenda?"

"Maybe..." Maddock said, "or maybe it has more to do with your pulse."

All he got was blank looks.

"When you get excited, or angry, or even happy, what happens to your heart rate?"

"It, uh, goes up," Bones replied, still not following.

"Exactly," Maddock said, thinking as he spoke.

"What if it can somehow detect your heartbeat. Maybe whoever made it didn't fully understand human anatomy. They may have seen a fast beating heart as angry or evil. Maybe its architects were naturally calm people." He looked at Bones when he said *people*. He knew his partner would understand the word's real meaning.

Aliens.

"Sounds like a longshot," Haugen said, never taking his eyes off the artifact. "Either way, you can count me out. I don't think I could handle such a burden."

Maddock looked at Bones who shook his head. "Nope...forget it."

Maddock sighed. He knew his pulse was as slow and steady as it always was. He'd have to do it. Donning a pair of thick winter gloves, he stepped up to the coffin, and without further thought, reached in, wrapping his hand around the midway point of the spear's shaft.

What happened next was unexpected.

TEN

It had been fifteen minutes since the three men entered the tomb and they'd yet to come out. Either they were dead, or intentionally delaying the inevitable. Death.

Hoor double-checked his weapon and stood from his kneeling position just around the bend in front of the cave entrance. He used it for cover, just in case the others came out firing. Moving quickly, he switched on his rifle's barrel-mounted light, and without pause, continued into the mountain, making his way deeper into the unknown.

He stopped and listened.

Silence.

Hoor started up again, doing what he could to resist running in with the trigger depressed. All he wanted was Gungnir. If he had to spray the tomb with bullets, he would. But as soon as he exited the tunnel, his jaw dropped. Fairhair's coffin was there, as was his treasure, but there was no sign of the three men who had gone in after it.

What of Odin's spear?

Practically leaping across the room, he found the crypt empty, save for the long-dead king's corpse.

Empty....

He spun and looked for the others. Nothing. Even Sorensen was gone.

Seething in anger, Hoor feverishly inspected every square inch of the tomb, eventually stumbling upon the hidden tunnel in its rear. Holding up his light, Hoor could barely see a few feet in front of his face, but he could hear them. Their footfalls echoed in the tight confines of the underground passage. He took a few strides forward and stopped when he saw a second tunnel on the left and a third to the right.

Which way?

A noise drew his attention back to the tomb as another set of footsteps could be heard, pounding down the entryway. Not knowing who it was, Hoor took up a firing stance behind King Harald's coffin and waited. Then, he saw them, three red lasers swaying back and forth in the dust-filled air.

ScanoGen's strike team.

Hoor stood and lowered the barrel of his *Heckler & Koch* MP5 submachine gun. The incoming team was earlier than he expected, throwing yet another monkey wrench into his plans. But, he knew with three armed men and a berserker on the run, having the extra firepower wouldn't be a bad thing to have. He'd need to be patient and wait for the right opportunity to steal away.

"You're early," he said to the six men. They formed a semi-circle around him, all standing as still as ghosts. Then, one of them stepped forward, his face hidden behind a pair of futuristic goggles.

"And you're late. Our employer isn't pleased." The team's commander looked at the others. "We aren't exactly cheap." The others laughed and grinned like schoolchildren. The bravado wasn't in short supply with this bunch. "Thankfully, he had us in the area just in case you screwed the pooch."

Hoor's face soured. Scano had such little faith in his work that he secretly sent a team in behind him as a backup plan. "Mr. Scano is impatient. I work slowly so I don't get myself killed. You, on the other hand, would rather barge into a monster's den, boots stomping as loud as cannon fire, guns hot." He smiled. "And believe me, I doubt any of you would've survived his fury."

"Give me a break, beanpole." The team leader stepped up beside the coffin. "Where's the artifact?"

"Taken, unfortunately."

"What?"

"Relax, Mr…"

"The name's Killian, but my associates here call me, Kill."

"Kill?" Hoor asked, resisting the urge to roll his eyes. "Okay then, Mr. Kill, they took the spear into the tunnels under the mountain. They shouldn't be too far ahead of you. I'll await your arrival outside and—"

"Not a chance, sonny boy." All six men leveled their assault rifles at Hoor. "You're going to lead the way." Kill stepped closer. "And if Mr. Scano doesn't get what he wants, I have orders to put a bullet in your brain, *capisce*?"

Knowing when he was outnumbered and outgunned, Hoor nodded and backed away toward the rear tunnel. As he moved off, he heard a rustling sound from just inside the entrance. Instead of waiting to see what it was, he took off running and was quickly met with shouted voices.

But there was also something else there too.

A low growling could be heard just under the men's voices. Hoor knew what it was and if his luck would have it, the six-man strike team would have their hands full with…

"*Ulfhednar*."

The berserker stepped out from a previously unnoticed alcove, flexing and straining against an invisible force. Luckily for Hoor, Sorensen didn't seem to notice him deeper within the shadows. He'd covered his flashlight with his free hand and flattened himself against one of the walls.

But the other men weren't so fortunate.

Eyes wide in terror and awe, Hoor witnessed the *hamrammr*, or *shapestrong*—a berserker who changed form—howl into the cave, rattling every bone in his body. Then, Sorensen's frame began to crack and break, growing larger and mightier as it did. The man's already huge physique became even more monstrous.

The *hamask*—the building internal rage—seemed to increase tenfold with every breath. Soon, the berserker would be at full-strength and unstoppable. Hoor had no intention of being around when it did. He'd be as dead as the strike team was about to be.

Gunshots reverberated and the creature bellowed in anger, charging straight into the cave with a flurry of sweeping blows. Shouts of surprise quickly turned into those of gargled agony as the hired professionals were swiftly slaughtered.

Hoor didn't stop running.

The only thing that would stop his pumping legs was the three men he sought, a dead end, or worse, the berserker. He knew the beasts could be injured, but could they be killed? The legends about them were written when sword and shield, bow and arrow were the primary implements of war. What about high-caliber, armor-piercing rounds?

A bloodcurdling roar stopped him in his tracks. That was when he realized that the shooting had stopped. The berserker lived, but was it well enough to hunt?

Hoor took off running again, refusing to answer his

own question. For the first time in years, he was truly terrified.

Sorensen's initial change was like nothing he'd ever felt before. His bones cracked and popped, elongating and thickening. Once he outgrew his clothes, they shredded to nothing. Hair—no, not hair, *fur*—sprouted all over his body. His already ample chest hair thickened and grayed.

His bushy beard fell out next and his already wild hair lengthened and grayed like the rest of the invasive coat. The color was something he recognized too. It was the same as the wolves in the region. He was becoming one of Odin's champions—his *Ulfhednar*.

Part of him was still there mentally while it all happened, crying out in fright as he became a monster. But there was something else inside him as well. He could feel a presence within his mind, pushing him to savagery, a primal instinct to fight and kill.

The *hamask* was alive and well in him, but if he concentrated enough, he could control it… To a degree. Seeing Henrik had loosened the blinding rage's hold on his mind some, returning a bit of his humanity with it. At first, he wanted to kill everyone in that tent, but when his friend's eyes met his, he instead felt a calling to protect them.

He felt it now, too.

Haugen and the two Americans had only just exited the tomb when a fourth man, someone who was after Gungnir for its abilities, entered. Sorensen was supposed to follow behind Haugen and the others but quickly decided to stay behind and fight. The worst thing that would happen is that he would die and his nightmare would be over. If he could take out the incoming force in the process, he was content with that.

Something shot past him in a blur as he hid. He thought about abandoning his post to pursue it, but rejected the idea, and stayed true to his original plan instead. Stepping into the cave once more, Sorensen saw six men holding assault rifles. Each and every one of them gawked at his hulking form, and as he attacked, each one sent their own barrage of gunfire his way.

Diving over the coffin, Sorensen rolled and leaped to his feet, slashing one of the gunmen with his dagger-like claws. Lifting the shooter off the ground, he violently impaled him into an overhead stalagmite. A horrible popping sound was accompanied by a sickening wetness as the stone growth burst through the now dead man's chest. Letting go, Sorensen noticed that the body didn't fall to the floor. Instead, it just slumped, seemingly hanging in midair.

A half-dozen rounds pierced his flesh. He was aware of the pain, a dull, distant thing, barely worth his notice. He wheeled around and lashed out, backhanding another of the mercenaries with such force that the blow broke the man's neck. The four remaining men backpedaled, watching in astonishment as the wounds Sorensen suffered quickly clotted, stemming the loss of blood to practically nothing. The wounds remained, the injuries did not heal instantly, but they no longer bled.

That made Sorensen smile. He'd do his duty and give Haugen and others the time they needed to escape. More deafening gunfire erupted, pushing Sorensen back some. But he fought the waves of pain and leaned into the volleys. When the men were obliged to stop shooting in order to reload, he made his move.

Diving forward, he rammed two of them, driving the

air from their lungs. One man broke his back against a column of rock. The other lived, but not for long. Pinning his next victim down, he gripped the killer's throat and squeezed, ending his life in seconds.

Two more left.

Leaping to his feet, Sorensen looked for the last two gunmen, but couldn't see them. He calmed his roaring rage, and listened, hearing their footfalls in the rear tunnel. They were attempting to flee in the same direction as the others. With a growl he vaulted over Fairhair's coffin, landing in a sprint on the other side.

Sniffing the air as he moved, Sorensen could smell blood in the dank corridor. The two he pursued were injured, giving him an easy-to-follow trail. It was another of his recently acquired traits. He could smell and hear everything around him. He grinned but just as quickly frowned. He was beginning to enjoy his newfound gifts.

They are not gifts… They are a curse.

But he knew he'd need to use them as though they were gifts, then… He didn't know. He felt another part of him begin to slip away after his last fury-induced change. Would he eventually become nothing more than a blood-thirsty monster in time, or could he continue to control it?

The growing scent of blood thankfully got his mind off the unnerving question. If he could, he'd take his own life.

Is it possible? He knew the berserkers of old were mostly immortal in battle when in their *hamask*—the fury-induced mental state. He clenched his fists but calmed at the thought. Was that the key to killing an *Ulfhednar*? If he calmed, could he be killed?

Just more questions.

The sound of gunfire ahead was answered with his own concussive roar. Somewhere ahead, Haugen and the others were in trouble. Sorensen picked up his speed and charged into the unknown. When he eventually exited the tunnel, he'd get a glimpse into the past—into something that must've come from the future.

Or another world…

Buried beneath the forests of Norway was the most unbelievable sight he'd ever seen. Not only was it an incredible find but it also gave him the answer to the question of who conceived Gungnir.

It was them, he thought, standing still in shock. *It was 'them.'*

ELEVEN

Maddock had come close to losing control, transforming into a berserker. Only his SEAL training had enabled him to avoid succumbing to fear. Like everyone else that made it through the rigorous program, he developed the uncanny ability to stay calm in every situation possible.

Possible... Right.

The tunnel exited into a massive cavern, the pathway holding straight and true. But it wasn't the yawning space that took his breath away. It was what filled that space.

Viking longships... *Metal* Viking longships. They lined both sides of the five-foot-wide footpath, beautiful in the eeriest of ways. Side by side in formation, the ships looked ready for battle, awaiting their crew. The bow's customary dragon head was nowhere to be found. Instead, there was a wickedly sharp protruding blade.

Maddock did his best to ignore them as he ran, but that was easier said than done. He had no doubt that these *ships* were made by a race other than human. Plus, keeping his mind off the spear he held was even more difficult. He soon discovered that analyzing the alien crafts helped keep his fear in check.

The Viking-style *starships* had neither sail nor mast. Instead, the center portion of each crafts' deck held an oblong dome, which Maddock assumed was the cockpit. Each ship was black as night but unique in design and shape, some being longer or taller. But they all stayed true to the classic long ship construction for the most part. Each was seamlessly built and perfect for their intended purpose.

Interstellar travel.

Bones was right.

The alloy it was made from was similarly incredible. The light from their flashlight did not illuminate the metal, but was absorbed deep into the material, swallowed by the impossibly dark material.

It occurred to Maddock that Gungnir was made of the same alloy. He imagined its surface felt unnaturally cold like some alloys did. Or, it could've just been his building fear, causing his mind to think such a thing. He possessed an alien weapon that had the capability to turn a human into a raging monster. All he had to do was lose it and he'd be one of them.

Sorensen....

The guy couldn't turn it off either. Even though he shrank back into his normal size, the beast within had still been there, waiting to be switched on again. It was also there externally. Becoming something else on the inside could be manageable—maybe. But being something different on the outside? Something inhuman? Maddock couldn't fathom that.

Bullets tore into the ground behind them, sending Maddock diving between the next two ships to his right. He came out of his roll with the spear in one hand and his gun in the other. Bones and Haugen did the same across the path, kneeling together, weapons at the low ready.

Feeling restrained by his puffy jacket, Maddock quickly shrugged out of it. Being able to move quickly was more important than staying warm at the moment. Seeing him ditch the coat, Bones and Haugen did the same.

"You can't run from me!" a voice shouted.

Hoor, Maddock thought, ripping one glove off so he could handle the pistol easier. He'd have to be even more careful now.

"All of this around you... It's my destiny. I will become the general of the most fearsome army in all the world—in all its history."

"Not gonna happen, little man!" Bones shouted, antagonizing the lunatic. He loved to piss off the enemy, trying to make them sloppy, acting with emotion instead of strategy. "All you're getting is a good old-fashioned beat down from yours truly." Bones glanced at Maddock and motioned with his chin to get going. He pointed at himself and Haugen and then the ground where they knelt. They were going to stay behind and give Maddock the time he needed to do... What exactly? Escape? Escape to where?

If, he made it out alive, where would he go? They were miles away from civilization and the terrain would still be cold and unforgiving. Then there were the wolves; Maddock knew there would be more of them. That was only one pack and he figured there'd be others.

Maddock shook his head. He wasn't going anywhere. They needed to give Sorensen more time. If what they knew about the berserkers was true, then they were confident in seeing the man again. Another stream of bullets tore into Maddock's hiding place, pinging off the long ship's hull, making him duck further away as a result. Hoor had them pinned down and was no doubt making his way to them with every volley thrown. Plus, what of the strike team?

"Run, dammit, run!" another voice shouted,

Maddock risked a look and saw two of the shooters

explode out of the entry like a pair of shotgun blasts. And from the look on their faces, something horrifying was chasing them.

Sorensen.

A monstrous roar echoed around them, reverberating back and forth as it made its way through the cavern. Neither of the soldiers stopped to help Hoor. They just blew by him and kept running. Whatever their services cost, it obviously wasn't enough for them to risk their lives.

Sorensen appeared and slid to a stop, his eyes darting around the room. His legs buckled and he fell to one knee in shock. Maddock chanced a second glance and was bowled into by one of the passing gunmen. Gungnir went flying, clattering off the stone path. Now, entangled with one of the mercs, Maddock struggled to get to his feet, trading blows the entire time.

The encounter seemed to bring the two gunmen to their senses. They stopped trying to run, and decided to turn and fight. One pulled a blade, the other a handgun. Maddock dodged a slash aimed at his throat and countered quickly, leaping forward. Now inside the man's reach, he sent a strong elbow into his face. Blood splattered from the man's nose, and he reared back in pain.

Bones and his opponent rolled past Maddock and his, the two men struggling to shoot one another. Bones' weapon was knocked out of his hand and he ducked a wild shot, quickly slapping the shooter's own gun away.

Standing tall, the two combatants sized each other up. Slowly and methodically, the assault team leader unsheathed his combat knife. Holding it up for Bones to see, he expertly flipped it into the air, catching it in a backhanded grip.

Shrugging, Bones yanked both of his hatchets free and flipped them in the air, letting them rotate a few times before skillfully catching them. The strike team commander gripped his weapon harder and attacked, slashing back and forth with the knife. Bones parried, with one axe, chopping with the other, but the man knew what he was doing. They parried back and forth, steel ringing and throwing of bright sparks, all the while gauging the other's abilities and fighting pattern.

Maddock saw little of this. His foe had retaliated and connected with a kick to his gut. Doubling over from the blow, Maddock caught an uppercut to the chin and went down. Despite seeing stars, he froze as a gun was leveled at his face.

But instead of getting shot point blank, the gunman jerked as if touched by a live wire, and then staggered forward, a hatchet buried between his shoulder blades.

Thank you, Bones, Maddock thought, regaining his equilibrium and kicking the dying man away to send him careening backward. The axe was pushed deeper into the man's back as he slammed into the longship behind him. Maddock just stayed rooted to the spot, breathing in deeply and collecting himself as the man slid down the longship and fell over in a heap.

Where's Haugen?

He turned away from the dead man and found Hoor standing over the prone police chief. He and the psychopath must've gotten into it while the two of them fought the specialists.

Without a hint of remorse, Hoor drew his pistol and pulled the trigger.

Haugen's lifeless eyes met Maddock's. The man was

gone—just like that.

"You bastard!" Bones shouted, burying his remaining axe in the team leader's skull in one savage move. Shoving the man away, Bones clenched his meaty fists and started toward Hoor.

But someone else got there first.

Sorensen leaped high into the air, easily clearing Maddock and Bones by twenty feet. As he fell in Hoor's direction, he threw his arms out wide, jaws agape. The fanatic simply knelt and closed his bare hand around Gungnir.

When Sorensen made contact, it wasn't with the frail, gun-toting lunatic from before.

It was with a second berserker.

An infinitely more frightening one.

While Sorensen's fur was wolf-grey, except where it was covered in blood, Hoor's was as black as Gungnir and the surrounding longships. It looked as if the evil within him was coming alive on the outside. Maddock groaned, knowing they were now horribly screwed.

The one thing that they could not let happen just had.

The little twit finally became the *god* he always dreamt of being. In true Viking fashion, he howled into the air like a warrior going *berserk* and attacked with the might of an ancient deity from hell. The blood of his enemies would flow freely, starting with Sorensen and the two Americans.

Sorensen's massive form fell like a missile and slammed right into Hoor, sending both berserkers tumbling further down the docking bay's central path. Maddock's attention was arrested by the sound of metal clinking on stone. Looking down, he found Gungnir laying not five feet away from him.

Without hesitation, he picked it up and regrouped with Bones, both men beaten and exhausted. With each passing second, Maddock felt a strange pulling sensation, as if something was trying to draw his soul out of his body.

Dammit, he thought, realizing it was the weapon reacting to his physical state. He needed to calm down before he changed. He ducked behind one of the longships with Bones, away from the savage battle taking place between the two berserkers. Closing his eyes, he willed his pulse to slow his, visualizing the influence of the spear retreating like an outgoing tide.

"You all right?" Bones asked, seeing his friend struggle.

Maddock softly nodded. "Sure, as long as I don't get too worked up."

Bones laughed. "Good luck with that."

The chuckled was short-lived when he remembered what happened to Haugen. "That asshole just stood there and put a bullet in his head." Grinding his teeth, he glanced back to Maddock who looked like he was about to pass out. "My bad, I'm just pissed is all. He was a good man."

Maddock nodded, trying not to let the sentiment trigger him.

"We need to go," Bones said, taking a quick look. "Back the way we came."

Their hiding spot was bashed into from behind, sending the longship screeching across the floor. Only his quick reflexes saved Bones from becoming a crimson stain. Diving out into the open, he rescued himself from certain death, only to leap right back into the path of it.

Hoor stood over him, his eyes bloodshot and manic. He was twitchy and drooling like a rabid dog, which wasn't too far from the truth. Sorensen had fought the changes, and in doing so, retained some of his humanity. Hoor, on the other hand, had embraced the transformation, losing himself in the process. There was no turning back for him.

Where is Sorensen? Maddock wondered as he dove into Bones, pushing him out of the way of Hoor's descending claws. They rolled together and then got up and ran, bolting for the tunnel entry. He prayed they could get there before Hoor figured out what they were doing.

They didn't.

The black-furred berserker leaped over them and landed in between them and their exit, forcing both men to skid to a halt. Neither had any weapons, except for Maddock who still held Gungnir. From what they'd seen so far, the spear had one ability, changing someone into a berserker. It didn't actually seem to do much else.

Suddenly, something yanked him from behind, spinning him around. It was Bones, shoving him back the other way. If they were to get out of the docking bay alive, it wouldn't be through the front door. They'd have to venture deeper into the cavern and hope to lose the beast there.

A blur of motion shot between them and slammed into Hoor like a battering ram. Sorensen jammed his claws into Hoor's chest and pushed, driving him further toward their original entrance, the entire time roaring for them to run.

They got another hundred feet when the path

forked. The left-hand route descended deeper into the underground world toward. The right-hand ramp inclined upward, hopefully toward the surface.

Hopefully.

TWELVE

"We've picked up movement in Vikersund."

Tam stopped pacing, and faced the technician who was bent over a laptop computer, a pair of noise-canceling earphones settled around his head. Nodding emphatically, the agent went on. "A small surgical team was spotted heading into the mountains a few hours after our boys."

Tam's face fell. "Holy sh—" She stopped herself, not wanting to make another deposit into her swear jar. But, she knew with a strike team inbound, she'd most likely be ponying up a hefty sum by the end of the day.

"Get boots on the ground, mine included," she calmly ordered. "We aren't losing civilians in the field." Not only were they civilians, but it was Dane and Bones. While *friends* were hard to come by in her line of work, Maddock's crew were some of the closest people to it. She'd hate to have to tell the others back home that they died on an op that she organized.

"Roger that," the agent replied, getting to work. "We're in the air in fifteen."

Tam headed for the apartment door, never looking back. "Make it ten."

She'd rented the ski lodge's uppermost floor a few days before with the intent of utilizing its rooftop feature. Helicopter tours were a popular attraction in the area. The surrounding fjords offered spectators a magical view for those willing to pay top dollar for the services.

Tam booked all the tours too. She and three others would board the chartered helo, disguising themselves as nothing more than American visitors. She'd even added a sizable bonus to keep the pilot's mouth shut should they need to land, something that was strictly prohibited.

Swinging open the front door, she crossed the hall and keyed open the neighboring room. Entering, she slammed it shut in frustration, leaning up against it. Closing her eyes, she took a moment to knead away a headache.

She'd need to be ready in five minutes. Thankfully, she was already dressed for an outdoor excursion, just in case. Tam believed in being ready for anything at any time. The only thing missing from her person was her gear, and she'd have to choose that carefully. They'd have to travel light in order to keep their cover intact. She had a small arsenal on hand, but openly carrying assault weapons would be a dead giveaway. On the other hand, if Maddock and Bones really needed her help… If whatever they had run up against was too big for them to handle, then showing up to the fight armed with pea-shooters wasn't going to do them any good.

She mentally went through every curse she could think of and promised herself to use the future swear jar money to buy the guys a few when they got back. *If they get back*, she thought, hating herself for not going with them. She trusted Maddock and Bones explicitly, but still preferred to stay in control whenever she could. Coordinating agents in the field remotely wasn't the same as true control, though. Whether they lived or died, she'd still be safe somewhere else, listening to their last breaths over their comms.

That was another problem. Maddock and Bones *weren't* linked with tactical comms units. Civilians didn't wear throat mics or have military-grade headsets. There was no body armor either. No, they were truly exposed and on their own.

Tam knelt at the foot of her bed and slid a large black suitcase from beneath it. It had a fingerprint scanner and a ten-digit combination lock. Quickly punching in the combo with her right hand, she depressed her left thumb on the scanning pad. A click answered the effort and she flung open the lid.

She allowed herself a smile upon seeing its contents—four Mark XIX Desert Eagle semi-automatic pistols, chambered for .50 caliber Action-Express rounds. She removed three of them, along with Kydex holsters, which she clipped onto her belt. The guns were heavy and awkward, but her coat concealed them from view.

"Thank the lord for poofy jackets," she said with a grin. Then she remembered why she was arming herself for war. If Maddock and Bones died in the field, she'd never forgive herself.

"We need to get the hell out of here, and fast!" Bones yelled, running for his life. He and Maddock ran for the right-hand ramp hoping it did, indeed, lead to the surface. Once there, they'd put their spy gear to use and call in for backup.

Hoor was after them again but Sorensen was dogging him every step of the way. The two beasts beat and clawed one another repeatedly, but neither could gain the upper hand. It was a stalemate. The legends seemed to be true; the berserkers were unkillable in battle.

But they were slowing. Neither was moving with their original fury. The injuries they suffered seemed to be having a cumulative effect on them, but they continued to fight, one trying to kill Maddock and Bones and the other doing what he could to prevent that from happening.

Maddock didn't respond to Bones' outburst, running alongside him in silence. His eyes were narrowed and focused, unwavering. Bones understood the silent treatment he was getting. The artifact in his partner's hands was lethal if activated and Maddock needed to keep his mind clear.

"We need to get that thing away from Hoor," Bones said, trying to turn the conversation around. He wanted to help Maddock anyway he could, but at the moment, he felt completely helpless. What could he realistically do?

Nothing, he thought, glancing over his shoulder.

Sorensen was riding Hoor piggyback-style, gnawing on the other man's shoulder meat, all the while yanking his foe further and further toward the left-hand ramp. He must've hit something vital because Hoor went down like a ton of bricks. But his reaction to the impact also threw Sorensen free. He rolled and landed hard on his back breathing heavily and panting, tongue lolling like a weary wolf.

Neither creature moved for a beat but Bones didn't slow, neither did Maddock. They continued up the incline. Bones legs were burning, his limbs like lead. His lungs felt like they were full of acid and he could taste blood in his mouth with every exhalation. He didn't know how much longer he could go on.

"Where do you think this goes?" Bones managed to gasp.

He turned back to Maddock, who just shrugged at first, but then he spoke. "Those longships would need a pretty big opening to get through to the hangar. I remember from the map that there's a small lake on the other side of the mountain. That could be our back door."

"So how do we open it?"

Maddock looked at Bones. "We'll find out when we get there."

That wasn't exactly comforting. For all they knew, when they found their exit, it might be impassable. *Or, maybe not*, Bones thought. The entrance hadn't been that difficult to get through. Just a simple iron gate guarding what lay within. Maybe the launch bay would be equally simple.

I guess we'll find out soon enough.

"Here," Maddock said, shrugging out of something across his back.

"Hell yes!" Bones cheered, taking the large splitting axe.

"Completely forgot I had it, not that it will do much against a berserker."

"Better than nothing," Bones said, grinning. "Being completely empty-handed isn't comforting. He glanced down at the spear. "Sorry, I didn't mean…"

"I know what you meant."

Maddock stumbled.

Bones grabbed his arm. "You good?"

Shaking his head, Maddock bit his lip in pain. "Gungnir, it's doing something to me. I feel… drained."

"Same here, bud."

Maddock looked at him hard. "Not *that* kind of drained."

"Oh… Okay. What then?"

Not having an answer, Maddock just shrugged out of

Bones' grip and continued forward but at a slower pace. Bones knew they needed to either ditch the spear or destroy it. It was apparently not meant to be carried around by human hands for so long. It was a weapon *for* berserkers. A human needed rest and sustenance to do so, neither of which was readily available. A berserker had the ability to heal and regain its strength.

And that was exactly what it was trying to do to Maddock; seducing him with the promise of unlimited strength and energy. Fighting that temptation was probably killing him.

"What do you think this place really is?" Bones asked, looking around. He noticed the berserkers had been left behind, hopefully descending deeper and deeper underground.

"If I had to guess," Maddock replied, struggling to speak, "I'd say it was an underground fortress of some kind. Or I guess *starbase* would be a better term." He cringed, gritting his teeth. "I have a sneaking suspicion that the hangar down there is only the tip of the iceberg."

"The other ramp?" Bones asked. "You think it leads down to some kind of alien stronghold, don't you?"

"What do you think?"

Bones shrugged. "Makes sense, I guess. But what I really want to know, is whether the complex is still populated or not."

"Well," Maddock said, sighing, "for our sake, let's hope not. We really don't need any more surprises."

THIRTEEN

The helicopter bearing Tam and her team hovered just offshore. They pretended to take in the sites, but what they were really doing was waiting. And hoping. They'd been airborne for twenty minutes and had yet to pick up on either of Maddock or Bones' GPS signals, which hopefully just meant they were still underground.

Ever since sending in her operatives, Tam had continued to dig for more information concerning the area. What she found was not terribly useful. There were stories of ancient armies marching through and descriptions of berserkers being used in battle in the country, but nothing that seemed particularly believable. Yet, considering what was contained in Sorensen's email, Tam was beginning to think those stories held some grain of truth that was tied to what Maddock and Bones now pursued.

The timing of the events was still something that didn't make sense to her, however. If it had taken Sorensen around two days of steady hiking to reach the tomb, how did he send an email and then quickly disappear in only a day? He would have had to have moved at incredible speed over rough terrain for an entire day without stopping.

It's not possible... Unless there's more going on than we originally thought.

Now, she couldn't help but question her decision to send in only two men. She could've at least armed them better and given them a better chance at survival. But she trusted their abilities. If there were ever two men that could handle whatever was thrown at them, it was Dane

Maddock and Bones Bonebrake. SEALs were in a class by themselves, able to take punishment, turn it around and dish it out. She'd seen it up close and in person before.

They'll make it.

"Anything yet?" she asked, glancing at her communications technician. Not taking his eyes off his equipment, he only shook his head in the negative.

Deciding to call an audible, Tam turned to the pilot from her co-pilot chair. "Take us north," she ordered. "Head for my people's last known position."

Landing and pursuing Maddock and Bones on foot was the next option. The pilot nodded and pushed the helo north. The helicopter began to climb as it passed over the center of town. Tam sat back and tried to relax. They must still be underground, she told herself, trying to believe it

The tomb was somewhere in the forest, sitting at around 1,000 feet in elevation. No one really knew what they'd find, but Tam's satellite map showed a small clearing a mile from where Maddock and Bones' signal disappeared.

Better than nothing.

Holding it up for the pilot to see, Tam tapped on paper, getting a wide-eyed look from the man.

"What is it?" she asked, curious. She thought she learned everything there was to know about the region. But from the pilot's reaction, there was obviously more to learn.

"That area is a dead zone," he explained. "I've heard stories. Some are pretty crazy, but the people who told them are completely sane."

"Stories?"

"Equipment failures. Electronics fizzling out for no reason. Compasses going screwy."

"Compasses?" Tam asked. "So, it's a geomagnetic phenomenon."

The pilot shrugged. "Could be. There are stories of people becoming lost because of it. I'm a little worried about flying in there if there's a chance that our systems could be affected. And then of course, there are the monsters. If you believe in that sort of thing." He chuckled but quickly stopped when he noticed that Tam wasn't laughing along.

"What if I did believe?"

His eyes narrowed unsure of what to make of the attractive African-American woman. "Just the ramblings of a drunkard. He's a local who lives way up the mountain—says there are ghosts that scare the wolves away from that spot."

A dead zone, Tam thought, watching the scenery fly by beneath them.

She'd heard of other places with that reputation. Allegedly, the Bermuda Triangle was one such. Strange things happened all the time there, and even with all the technology in the world, there was no consensus as to its cause. Like this place, the problem seemed to be related to the Earth's magnetic fields, but scientists could not provide empirical evidence for it.

"I don't care what's there," Tam said. "Just get us there."

Further down the decline, Sorensen and Hoor fought a running battle. They stumbled into a vast open cavern filled with a network of floating platforms connected by ramps and bridges. Entangled, the two berserkers rolled onto one, which held a single descending ramp at its center and bridged paths radiating out in every direction.

Momentarily pinned by Hoor, Sorensen pushed with all his might, forcing the larger beast off of him. Wriggling out, he stood only to take a swipe from Hoor's massive claws across his face. He cried in pain, feeling his right eye swell up with the trauma. Half-blind, Sorensen threw himself into Hoor, knocking them both from the landing.

The berserkers fell through open space. More platforms like the one they had just fallen from flashed past, but there was nothing directly below them except a long fall to the bottom. Sorensen lashed out and caught the edge of a platform. Warm blood oozed from the ragged, throbbing hole in his face. Doing his best to shut it out, he rolled himself onto the large slab of stone and collapsed onto his back. There he rested and took in his surroundings.

There was no sign of Hoor. If he had fallen all the way down and survived—and that seemed the most likely outcome—it would take a while for him to ascend the ramps. Beyond the platform, there was only darkness. Growling in discomfort, Sorensen sat up and spotted something on the platform with him. It was an odd-looking wedge of the alien black metal, standing upright like some kind of marker signpost.

Sorensen got to his feet and stumbled toward it. His legs gave out and he staggered forward, catching himself on his hands. One palm hit the surface of the metal, evoking an immediate response. Like a sleeping computer screen, it winked awake in a series of blue flashes. Then images began appearing just below its surface—no, not images… Schematics.

It's a map of the facility. He grinned as he saw familiar symbols marking the various levels. *And it's in the same language as the journal.*

Running a clawed finger across the map, Sorensen took in as much knowledge of the complex as he could. Knowledge was power and knowing the place's layout could be key to their survival.

His finger stopped when he read the name to the level he now stood on. Just then, a familiar fury-laden roar resonated from somewhere below his position, starling him momentarily. Hoor was still alive. He returned his attention to the map, reading the descriptions of each platform. The place held many secrets. If he and the others could make it back down here, they might be able to find a way to kill the creature, but no mortal weapon was going to kill Hoor. Instead, they would need to find an *immortal* weapon.

The path did not lead Maddock and Bones to an exit. Instead, it simply ended at the base of a massive wall of the jet black mystery metal. There were no seams that might have hinted at a secret door, nor any locks, handles, or a control mechanism. It was just a big wall of nothing.

"Do we knock?" Bones asked, keeping an eye on their rear. The two berserkers were still missing, presumably wreaking havoc on the lower levels of the alien compound.

"And risk touching it?" Maddock replied, shaking his head. "There has to be a way out of here. Why build a ramp to nowhere, it makes no sense?"

"So, what then?"

Maddock scratched his head. "No idea."

Bones pointed to the spear. "What about that?"

"What about it?"

"What if it acts as a key or something?" Bones asked. "It's worth a shot."

Maddock didn't argue. He knew anything was possible when it came to advanced tech. If a spear had the ability to change a person into a monster, why couldn't it do something as simple as opening a door? They were, after all, made of the same metallic material.

Stepping closer to the wall, Maddock held out the weapon.

Nothing.

He moved closer and this time, touched the tip to the surface.

A vibrant tracery of blue lines bloomed to life like a grid on a computer's motherboard. Energy pulsed from where the spearhead contacted it, causing the surface of the wall to ripple like the surface of a pond disturbed by a cast stone.

"Holy crap," Bones muttered.

Maddock backed away, feeling similarly awed. He could feel the wall buzzing with electricity, faint wisps brushing his face and tugging his hair.

"Static?" Bones asked before Maddock could.

"Looks like it... An electrical discharge or something."

A hiss of air startled the men, making them jump back. The hiss became a loud hum. The wall remained but now there was a vertical seam running up the middle. Then came a resounding *thunk* and then the seam parted, the separated halves sliding away from one another.

"Hangar doors for the longships," Maddock

muttered.

Daylight poured through opening… Followed by a crashing helicopter.

FOURTEEN

The two men dove to the ground as the out-of-control aircraft sailed overhead. Its tail rotor clipped one of the still retracting hangar doors and came apart, hurling shrapnel in every direction as the helicopter began to autorotate. Covering their heads, Maddock and Bones didn't see the crash, but they certainly heard and felt it.

After a few seconds however, silence settled in.

Uncovering their heads, Maddock and Bones got to their feet. The helicopter had come to rest fifty feet down the sloping ramp. It lay on its side, completely mangled but mostly intact.

"Whoever's in there got lucky," Bones murmured. "It could've been a hell of a lot worse.

A loud squeal broke the still and a door on what was not the top side was flung back. A figure appeared there and climbed out unsteadily, practically falling to the floor of the ramp. Recovering quickly, she stood up, faced the two awestruck men and grinned.

"Tam?" Maddock asked, confused but happy to see her.

"That was about as *Hollywood* of an entrance as I've ever seen," Bones said, moving to the woman. "I give it two thumbs up."

"Damn straight." Tam winced, apparently thinking of the swear jar in her office, to which she now owed another dollar. "I do all my own stunts," she retorted, then became serious. "The others…"

"On it," Bones said, and quickly scrambled up to the door she had just come through.

Maddock stayed with Tam. He was about to brief her

on what had happened so far, but then twin roars echoed up from the depths below.

"We need to leave."

"How exactly?" Bones asked from above, helping a stunned man—Tam's comm tech—out of the downed aircraft. "You just wrecked our ride."

"She most certainly did," complained another man who popped up beside the first.

"Let me guess," Bones said, helping the man down, "you're the pilot."

"And the owner...." He looked down sourly at the wreckage. "Former owner, I suppose."

"It'll be all right," Tam said. "You'll be generously compensated."

"If we live," Bones added, making sure the pilot understood the gravity of the situation. "If I were you, I'd be less worried about the insurance claim, and more worried about dying."

"Dying?" he asked.

"Painfully," Bones replied. "Gruesome even."

"That's enough," Maddock ordered, getting a wink from his partner.

Two more figures emerged from the helicopter—Tam's hired guns—both having escaped serious injury despite the rough landing. Maddock's crew had quickly gone from two to seven, all armed. Tam supplied the civilian pilot with a standard issue service pistol. She then unzipped her coat and showed Maddock and Bones her *goods*.

"Hey, now..." Bones said. "At least let me buy you a drink first."

Rolling her eyes, she drew back her coat to reveal the weapons.

"Desert Eagles?" Bones noted, one eyebrow raised skeptically. "People might think we're compensating for something." He glanced over at Maddock. "Especially you."

Tam shook her head in mock despair and then handed over the enormous pistols, along with spare magazines. "I figured if you guys were having *this much* trouble, you'd need a little extra firepower. But if you don't want them—"

"Oh," Bones interrupted, "I'm not complaining. You're right about needing extra firepower."

Another set of roars underscored the statement.

"We have to go down there," Maddock declared. "Unfinished business."

"ScanoGen?" Tam asked.

"Um, no…" Bones said. "Long story short, Scano was never getting what he wanted."

"Is that it? Gungnir?" Tam said, staring wide-eyed at the weapon in Maddock's hand.

Maddock nodded. He quickly related everything that had happened, and then added, "We need to kill the berserkers and figure out a way to destroy this thing."

"Destroy?" she asked. "But—"

"No buts," Maddock said sharply. "This thing is a game changer in every meaning of the word. *No one* needs this kind of power."

Bones stepped up next to him. "Absolutely no one."

Biting her lip, Tam considered the ultimatum, and then finally nodded. "Fine, I believe you."

"Then let's do this." Maddock noticed that no one had argued his use of the word, *berserkers*. Plural. As in both of them.

Sorensen would also have to be eliminated.

He'd want it that way.

There was blood everywhere, coating every surface of the lower ramp. The amount spilled should have exsanguinated ten of the creatures let alone two. The coppery aroma filled the air.

"I don't see how bullets are going to stop anything that can bleed this much and still be alive," Tam said.

She'd stuck to Maddock's side since they began their descent, coaxing as much information out of him as possible. Unfortunately for her, neither he nor Bones knew much.

Even after retrieving a journal belonging to Sorensen's ancestor, they were still in the dark. Apparently, the only one within the facility to read the ancient glyphs was now one of the berserkers. And from what Maddock described when talking to the *man*, Tam wasn't so sure he'd be any help.

"His mind is failing, turning feral," Maddock said, speaking quietly, describing his encounter within the tomb. "He was having trouble remembering basic vocabulary, something someone with his intellect shouldn't forget so easily."

"So, you really think it's a virus of some kind?" Tam asked.

Maddock shrugged. "As soon as Sorensen and Hoor touched the spear, they changed into berserkers. I can't imagine any ordinary virus working that fast, but we know it's made of an alien alloy. Maybe there's an alien virus, too. We don't even know what the spear's original purpose was."

"Original purpose?"

He nodded. "What its designers really intended it to

do. I can't imagine it did the same thing to them that it does a human. It doesn't make sense."

"I got it," Bones said, listening in on their conversation. He was on Maddock's right, keeping watch. "What if the Norse gods were actually aliens from another world? And I'm not talking Thor and Asgard—nothing like the movies. I'm talking *real* extraterrestrial type stuff, not Chris Hemsworth with shoulder drapes."

Maddock nodded thoughtfully. This certainly wasn't the first time they'd encountered ancient alien tech. "So, you think the stories about Odin and Gungnir—this," Maddock held up the spear, "were real?"

Bones shook his head. "Not the gods we've learned about. Sure, they may have inspired the legends, but not in the ways we've read about. There's something darker going on here."

"It certainly seems more sinister than what the Atlanteans were up to," Tam said.

"It's a weapon that can change a person into a rampaging monster," Maddock said, thinking aloud. "And we just so happen to have found it in the crypt of a king who was said to use it for his own benefit." He glanced to Bones and Tam. "That can't be a coincidence."

"No," Bones said, "it can't." His eyes opened wide. "Harald Fairhair was one of them. He was an alien—maybe one of the last ones. He used Gungnir to turn people into his warriors—his berserkers. He wanted an army of his own."

"Just like Hoor," Maddock added, nodding his agreement. "Makes sense, I guess. Not exactly easy to prove, though."

"I know," Bones said, "but just think about it. If you

were the last of your kind and you had the ability to repopulate the world with your own species, wouldn't you try? Fairhair—or Odin, I guess—built the spear with the intent of reviving his doomed civilization."

"What of his human remains?" Maddock asked,

"And that he existed on this planet for eighty years and then suddenly died," Tam said, trying to keep the conversation grounded.

"Who says it was his human followers who interred him here." Maddock and Tam stopped and faced Bones. He continued. "Do we know that the body up there was laid to rest exactly when Fairhair supposedly died? Remember what Haugen said…" The two men looked at each other, hurt in their eyes. "He said that most think Fairhair was buried somewhere else—Haugesund, I think it was called. What if someone else is there instead of the god-king."

"He could've come back here and continued his work in peace," Maddock replied, nodding his head. "And like dinosaurs, just because his skeletal structure was human in design, doesn't mean he actually looked like one."

"Exactly!" Bones said, getting amped.

"And Hoor?" Tam asked. "Where does he fall into this?"

"He's just some clown with a demented lust for power," Bones said continuing forward again. "Seems he bit off more than he could chew."

"What makes you say that?" Maddock asked.

Bones stopped again as the ramp leveled off. Stepping around his much bigger partner, Maddock's mouth opened to speak but nothing came out. Black fur, some of it still attached to layers of skin, lied in heaps all over the—

"What is this place?" Tam asked, equally shocked at the sight.

With one hand, Maddock held the spear against one of his shoulders, keeping it away from his vulnerable face. Next, he drew his heavy hitting Desert Eagle and breathed. Firing the .50 caliber weapon with one hand wasn't advisable—ever. Its recoil could, and most likely would, break his wrist if fired without the support of a second hand or specialized brace.

"Let's hold up here a minute," he said. "I need both hands. I'm going to strap the spear to my back."

"Need some help?" Bones asked.

"Probably better if you don't get too close to it."

"No argument from me on that."

As Maddock worked, the others looked around the lab facility. The rotten bodies littering the examination tables disturbed him deeply. Not only was this place Fairhair's base of operations, but part of it also doubled as a surgical suite.

"He tested it on people before it was ready," Maddock said, his voice choking with emotion.

Suddenly, a roar erupted from around the corner, followed by a mangled body—Sorensen's. It hit one of the tables and flipped over it, spilling whoever was already on there.

"What the…" Bones couldn't get the expletive out. The sight of Hoor stepping out of the shadows was too awful a sight to speak. But the discarded fur made perfect sense. It hadn't ripped away from his body during combat.

He shed it!

"What is he now?" Maddock asked.

"A god!" Boomed an all too familiar voice, accompanied by

Heavy footfalls the arrival of the booming voice's owner and once he fully came into view, everyone not changed into a berserker took a large step backward.

"Hoor?" Maddock asked, looking up at the twelve-foot-tall behemoth.

Smiling, the large being showed off a row of ultra-sharp fangs. His skin was still the pinkish hue of a human's but looked leathery and tough. Two large, solid black eyes stared back unblinking, looking very much like the classic gray alien from science fiction lore. His body was well proportioned, not as thick or bulky as a berserker's, but well-defined, with rippling muscles and ropes of sinew.

"He's a mix of human and alien," Bones said in awe. He'd always been fascinated with the subject. "You're one of them now, aren't you?"

"I am who I was meant to be," Hoor said. "Evolution at its finest. My royal blood deems me worthy." His shark-like gaze turned on Maddock. "I'll be needing *my* spear."

Maddock took another step away from the beast. "The owner of this weapon is dead. Odin is long gone."

"Odin?" the creature asked.

"The one and only," Bones replied, running with their earlier findings, not caring if they were a hundred percent accurate or not. "We figured out that Fairhair was an extraterrestrial and responsible for the legend. The Norse gods were frauds. They weren't gods at all, just beings from another world."

Hoor snarled as if offended by the notion that his ancestral gods were aliens and not spiritual beings. But then he smiled a few moments later. "I always knew I was special—my grandfather told me so." His eyes hardened again. "I am the last known descendant of Harald Fairhair, and therefore—"

"So, that's why you look the way you do," Bones interrupted.

He probably meant it as a taunt, but Tam picked up the thread. "While most humans reject the virus, turning into berserkers, your wretched DNA turns you into an abomination from outer space."

The rage of the twelve-foot giant bellowing into the air was like a volcano blowing its top. The room shook, sending racks of unidentifiable surgical equipment crashing to the floor. Maddock's team dodged additional debris as it rained down from the unseen ceiling above.

Maddock shook his head. "Way to go… You had to go and antagonize him, didn't you?"

Hoor began advancing. One of his steps equaled three of theirs. He was already almost close enough to reach down and rip the weapon from Maddock's back, though in all likelihood, he would probably tear *through* him to get it.

But then in a blur of motion, a half-dead Sorensen appeared between them, and rammed into and over Hoor, knocking him to the floor. The former school teacher then plucked Maddock from the others, threw him over his shoulder, and took off deeper into the complex much to the chagrin of the others.

Tam was about to give the order to open fire, but Bones stepped in front of her and grabbed her arm. "He may not look like it but Sorensen knows what he's doing. Plus," he watched as they and Hoor disappeared into the dark, "I'd really hate to hit my boy."

They all leaped back as Hoor climbed to his feet, but instead of going after them, he turned and pursued Maddock and Sorensen.

"What do we do?" Tam asked, feeling deflated.

"Not sure." Bones looked around at the room. They were in the center aisle. Off to each side were row upon row of operating tables, every single one of them full. Dark brown stains covered the floor beneath them all too. From the looks of it, the lab had been abandoned for some time.

"Why did Fairhair give up on his experiments?" Bones asked himself, saying it aloud. "Was it because he was dying or did he hit a biological snag?"

"Fan out and secure this room," Tam ordered her men, watching the three agents scatter. She then stepped up next to Bones. "What are you getting at?"

Bones turned and faced her, having to look down at the five-and-a-half-foot woman. "What if the berserker transformation is a negative reaction to his people's technology?"

"So, the berserker warriors were failed attempts at something greater?"

Bones nodded. "You heard what Mr. Hyde said… I've been thinking, why make them into gods if you're going to just send them into battle? It makes no sense unless you were hoping to get lucky and find one of your relatives." He motioned around the room. "They can obviously die too. We just need to figure out how to kill them."

"What happens if they continue to evolve?" Tam wondered aloud.

"Evolve?" the pilot asked, standing next to the nearest table.

"Don't look at me. It's what the hairless berserker said."

"They don't look evolved to me." He tilted his chin at the specimen.

Bones and Tam joined him and were immediately taken aback by the scene. Whatever it once was, the body was crippled and bent in all directions. It looked like its bones were twisted and broken before it was eventually killed.

"It was tortured," he said, frowning in disgust.

"What's your name?" Bones asked. The pilot looked capable enough. He was in great shape and had a face that said he'd seen action before. *Possibly ex-military*, Bones thought, examining the man. *Doesn't mean he was a foot soldier, though.*

"Max Neilson," he replied, still eyeing the corpse.

"Well, Max, we need everyone here to keep it together. If you're about to go bat-shit crazy on us, don't. I don't think I can handle Tam over there by myself."

Smiling, Max turned to Bones. "Only if you put in a good word with her for me."

Now, it was Bones' turn to smile, even chuckling a little. He was exhausted and laughing, if only a little, felt great. Slapping the shorter man's shoulder, they turned around together. "I'll see what I can do."

"Do what?" Tam asked, arms crossed. She heard everything and wanted to see what the two men would come up with to get out of the situation. Surprisingly, it was Max that spoke first.

"Well, I was curious if you were free for dinner later."

Bones probably expected Tam to kick the crap out of him, or, at the very least, chew him out. But instead, all she did was smirk and walk away, speaking over her shoulder as she did. "Let's get to work, shall we? If we can't figure out a way to stop Hoor, we're going to have to do it the old-fashioned way."

"And that is?" Max asked, looking at Bones.

The bigger man held up his index finger, opening and closing it several times. "A heavy dose of trigger finger workouts."

FIFTEEN

Having lost Hoor a few minutes ago, Sorensen set his human burden down, scouted the immediate area, and then collapsed. Maddock did what he could to help the man sit up, positioning him against a large, square metal container. They'd moved chaotically through a series of platforms and ramps, doing what they could to lose their pursuer. Feeling safe, Maddock took a moment inside what looked to be a storage warehouse of some kind.

And it was huge.

Indy, eat your heart out, he thought, checking to make sure they were alone. Once he confirmed that they were, he turned his attention to Sorensen.

The man looked terrible. He was missing his right eye, much like Odin, who according to Norse myth, sacrificed his eye in order to gain more knowledge of the world beyond. Sorensen, however, had given his eye to protect him and the others.

"Thank you," Maddock said softly.

Sorensen just sat there breathing hard, covered in blood. The fact he was still alive gave even more credence to the berserker legend. They truly were unbeatable in war. But if that was true, then Hoor was too.

"Is there a way to stop Hoor?" Maddock asked, hopeful.

"Yes," Sorensen replied, grunting out the word.

"How?"

Opening his good eye, Sorensen looked up at Maddock. "Weapons like Gungnir have such power."

"There are more of them?" he asked, a feeling of

dread washing over him.

"No, not like Gungnir," he replied, his Norwegian accent as strong as ever, "but, yes, there are others. They're each unique in design, built for a purpose."

Maddock about to ask for more information, but it occurred to him that Sorensen's speech had improved. "You're speaking well."

Sorensen nodded. "After my last change, I felt something inside ease. My mind and body are becoming one, accepting one another. I've also acquired an understanding of what I am now."

"You're in control?"

He nodded. "Some, yes, but the fury inside is still there. It's what drives me now. It keeps me vigilant."

"You said you have an 'understanding.'" Maddock reached his hand up and tapped what appeared to be a label on the container at Sorensen's back. "These are Norse runes."

Sorensen nodded. "In a way. It is this civilization's language—Fairhair's and those who came before him. I can read everything here. It's a more complicated version of what I'm used to, but still legible if I take it slow. I've learned much in only the short time I've been here. Between the journal and this place, I've gotten a good, hard look into their history... And their cold-hearted methods."

"So," Maddock said, realizing why they were really there, "you came to this storage warehouse on purpose. You know what's kept here."

Grunting, Sorensen stood and leaned against the large metal crate. "I found a map of the entire facility. This," he motioned to the space around them, "is mostly armaments."

Maddock softly whistled in amazement, slowly turning and taking in the massive room. "A weapons depot?"

"Yes, among other things."

"And you know what's needed to kill Hoor?"

He nodded, wincing as he involuntarily blinked his ruined eye. "Yes, it's the reason they couldn't be killed in battle. No human possessed a powerful enough weapon. They were hidden down here for the use of Odin's future army—"

"An army he never got to use."

"Exactly," he said, impressed with Maddock's quick understanding. "The technology that gives them their power also has the ability to take their lives."

"The alien metal."

"Yes, it's what they constructed their weapons out of, and if we can find the correct container, we can find the rest of the berserker army's arsenal. It's the only chance we have to end this." He went to step away from Maddock but stopped. "Both Hoor and myself…"

The finality in his statement hit Maddock hard. Sorensen wanted to die when it was all said and done. Unlike Hoor, he had no aspirations of becoming a god. His life had ended when he tried taking the spear.

But it didn't, Maddock thought, *and now he's living with the nightmarish consequences.*

"What about one of these?" Maddock asked, drawing his large handgun. "They didn't have this kind of firepower back then."

"It could work, but I'd like to be prepared if it doesn't."

Maddock understood that for sure. Over-preparedness always trumped the other option. Always.

Something still bothered Maddock. If Sorensen was in control and so was Hoor, what was the difference in their physical changes. Sorensen looked the same as before. He'd yet to shrink down—if it was even possible anymore. But Hoor, he…

"Tell me about Hoor's new form. Do you know why it happened?"

Sorensen stopped and faced Maddock, his permanently sour expression expanding more. "As much as I can figure, while I reject and fight what is happening to me… What *has* happened to me… He accepts it and embraces it, driving it deeper down within. Plus, his familial relationship to Fairhair."

"Regardless of if he's Fairhair's descendant or not, it doesn't surprise me," Maddock added, looking around. "He was obsessed before he changed. I'd imagine he's so far gone that there's nothing human left within him. He honestly thinks himself to be a god now. The ecstasy he felt when grasping the spear must've been indescribable."

"What about you?" Maddock asked. "How did you send an email after you first changed?"

"I…" he replied, thinking. "I don't remember a lot of what happened initially. When I first grasped the spear, I changed into a beast. But when I calmed, I mostly reverted back to my original form—yet I retained some of my newfound abilities." He stretched his shoulders, cringing as he did. "I tried to warn someone but was too scared to face anyone. After I sent it, I traveled as fast as I could back to the tomb."

Maddock gave him a minute to relax his thoughts. He didn't want to push it but time was short and Sorensen's intel was crucial. He ran his hand over the smooth surface of a nearby container. "Tell me about the other berserker weapons."

"Not much to say," Sorensen replied, still searching. They stayed in the center aisle, never venturing down any of the storehouse's other rows. "From what the research in the journal stated, they were ordinary in design but otherworldly in terms of ability. There are axes and swords and shields—"

"Any of them have effects like Gungnir?"

"Power? Yes. They have the might of many men within them, but only Gungnir, as it seems, has the ability to mutate another living being—human, or otherwise."

Maddock was relieved. The last thing they needed was another weapon like Odin's spear. It was constructed to build an army and start a war. The others were designed to be tools of that war.

"Over here…"

Maddock turned and found Sorensen standing off to the left staring at a wall. His mouth was slowly and silently opening and closing, speaking to himself. He was carefully translating a label filled with more of the space-aged Norse runes. Not voicing his question as to why Sorensen was trying to read a wall, Maddock instead made his way over to him, stopping when he saw it. The wall wasn't a wall at all, it was a container.

And it was huge.

"Whoa…" He craned his head up, having to bend backward at the waist to see it in its entirety. The thing had to have been eighty feet wide by another forty tall. "Is that—"

"Yes," Sorensen replied, exhaling hard. He reached out a hand. "Step back."

Maddock did and, just like he'd done with Gungnir,

he watched as Sorensen placed his hand on a seemingly random spot. But as soon as he made contact with it, it began to glow blue. Then, a grid network similar to what they'd seen at the hangar door appeared and spread across its surface.

Maddock realized that Sorensen's berserker DNA allowed him access to the otherwise forbidden area, controlling the mechanics within. All that was needed was a gentle touch.

The room shook slightly as the container's doors opened, retracting away from one another in sections. Stepping forward, Maddock pulled out his small flashlight but there was no need for it. A similar blue light illuminated the container's interior from above, casting the space in an eerie, ghostly aura.

"Okay then," he murmured as he beheld the contents.

Eight rows of shelves, ten feet apart from their neighbors came into view. Each held a variety of weapons, all perfectly stacked or racked depending on their construction and size, perfectly inventoried in their proper spot. On his right were large double-sided axes, very Viking in appearance. *Probably where the tribes of the region got their influences from as well.* It wasn't just their culture or belief system, they also styled their warring tactics and equipment after them.

Except these are hundreds of years old, maybe older.

Maddock headed for the middle aisle, finding it well-organized and dust free. The containers were airtight apparently, preserving their contents like they were just manufactured.

Curious, Maddock headed deeper into the storage unit. A secondary space lay beyond the rear of the shelving units, but held only a single object, a single six-foot-long container that looked almost like a sarcophagus.

But why...?

Maddock placed both hands on it, finding grooves in which to lift. He did, bending with his knees, driving the amazingly-modern, hydraulic lid up. A pressurized hiss answered as a seal was broken. It was followed immediately by a cloud of cold air, giving him another set of goosebumps as it kissed his skin.

Maddock was speechless. Inside lay a massive broadsword, five feet in length from pommel to tip. Its blade was what caught Maddock's attention, though. Not only was it made of the same black alien metal, but it seemed as if...

"It's moving," Maddock whispered.

He watched it as the blade's surface rolled and moved like it was partially liquid. He went to pick it up but paused and looked back at Sorensen. The berserker nodded his encouragement, wide-eyed. Breathing deep, Maddock gripped its hilt and stopped, feeling something odd. It wasn't pain or any other discomfort—nothing like Gungnir at all.

It was power.

Lifting it, he was blown away by how light it was. There was no way a sword of that size should've weighed so little.

"*Skofnung...*" Sorensen said with a far-off look, reading the engraving on the case. "It is the legendary sword of King Hrolf Kraki. Stories boast of its supernatural strength. Its other qualities are also quite fitting considering where we are."

"And what's that exactly?"

"Skofnung was said to be imbued with the souls of the great king's bodyguards. It was said that death couldn't deny its might."

"Bodyguards?" Maddock asked.

"*Berserker* bodyguards."

Shrugging, Maddock found the blade's scabbard and secured it around his back. With a .50 cal on his thigh and a haunted sword on his back, he was beginning to feel confident in what lay ahead. He would combine a weapon from Norse mythology with that of modern technology. At least one of them had to do the job.

Satisfied, they headed back to the front of the container, glancing back and forth between each row. Stopping at the collection of double-bladed axes, Maddock pulled two of them free and tossed them to Sorensen. They were huge, perfect for someone of Sorensen's size, but like Skofnung, they were easy to handle. The larger man caught them, spinning each like a twirler does batons. As each axe rotated, it sparked to life, igniting in a shower of crackling blue energy.

The big guy smiled and stood tall, ready.

Next was a collection of spears, each resembling Gungnir. Reaching out tentatively, Maddock calmed himself, expecting a taste of the same seductive berserker power, but felt nothing at all like that.

It was quite the opposite actually. The other berserker spear seemed to give him an extra boost—an oomph he desperately needed. He felt more and more refreshed with every second he held it.

It was another ability, one he could use too.

Thank God. The last thing he needed was another weapon trying to rip his soul apart. *But is that a good thing?*

He knew the consequences of relying on an object of such power. Like a pistol, these weapons gave their user a false sense of strength and security. Once done with a battle, a warrior would just go back to being a person, nothing more. It was the same with soldiers. While highly skilled on their own, they were still only as good as their tech in some cases.

Unless you properly honed those abilities when unarmed.

He and Bones could do plenty with their bare hands, using whatever they happened to have in front of them as a weapon, like in Henrik jr.'s store.

Henrik, dammit…

But in a war against a monster like Hoor, having alien tech on your side certainly couldn't hurt. Getting an idea, Maddock added Gungnir into the cluster of horizontally stowed spears. As soon as it was locked in place, even he couldn't tell the difference.

"Do you think Hoor will find it?" Sorensen asked as they left, stepping out and sealing the weapons vault with another touch of the metal.

Maddock looked up at him. "If you believed yourself a god, would you even go looking for it? He may need it down the road, but I doubt he'd go searching for it until we're all dead."

"Let's hope you're right."

SIXTEEN

We're getting nowhere with this," Tam said, rubbing her eyes hard. She and the others scoured the lab clean, looking for anything that could help them defeat Hoor. So far, all the tech was over their heads. Even the things they thought they recognized were no hope. Everything was in a language none of them spoke.

"Too bad Haugen isn't here," Bones said from behind. "Maybe he'd be able to help."

"Who?" Tam asked.

"Henrik Haugen, Chief of Police in Vikersund. He helped us find this place. He was a good guy."

"Was?"

Bones nodded. "Hoor shot him point blank in the head before going berserk. He was innocent and just doing us a favor. We sort of saved his son earlier and he offered to help us go after the people who were responsible."

"It was his duty," Tam countered. "He knew the risks."

"Getting chased by a crazed psychopath while in possession of an alien doomsday weapon was hardly Haugen's job. He's dead because of us."

"No," Tam said, "it's because of me. I asked you to come here alone. You did what you were trained to do, survive. You were severely outmatched and underinformed. If anyone is to blame for your friend's death, it's me."

"You're right, it's your fault," he said. As her eyes widened in surprise and dismay, he went on. "Or... We could just blame the bastard that killed him."

"Look," Max put in. "I may not be a professional or whatever you people are, but I know what murder is. This guy, Hoor, took the life of an innocent man. He needs to be put down *Old Yeller* style."

Bones smiled. He was starting to enjoy having the pilot around. But then he had also thought the same about Haugen. Getting too close to people was a bad thing in their line of work—a sin. Especially civilians with little or no training. And even worse when it was in as hostile an environment as now. He, Maddock, and even Tam knew the consequences. They could die at any time. It was a part of the gig. They had plenty of close calls over the years and every single time things went FUBAR, the prospect of death was also a potential outcome.

"Ugh," Max said, reeling back from something.

"What is it?" Bones asked.

"Not sure, but whatever it was, it looks like it was overcooked. Like a piece of meat was left on the grill for a month."

As Bones neared the man's position, he saw it too. A vaguely human form, but shrunken and twisted, and coal black. Max was right. Whatever happened to the test subject, it was burnt to a crisp.

"Huh…" Bones murmured, kneeling. There was an ashy residue on the ground surrounding the stomach-high examination table.

"What are you thinking?" Tam asked, circling the scene.

Groaning at what he was about to do, Bones reached down and swiped a finger through the soot. Lifting it to his nose, he sniffed and rubbed the debris between his thumb and forefinger

"Strange," he said, inhaling again. "It's definitely ash but there's an underlying trace of something else too."

"Might be a chemical of some kind," Tam suggested. Even though centuries had passed, disturbing the ash had released a distinctive and almost familiar chemical odor. "Maybe an accelerant."

Bones shook his head. "No, I don't think so. It smells more like ozone. I think the body was fried by an electrical discharge."

"He was struck by lightning?" Max asked.

Bones stood, wiping the ash on his pant leg. "I doubt it."

"What then?"

Bones looked down at the pilot. "I think it's this place. It's powered by a strange form of electrical energy. Whatever power source the beings here used is still active. They could've weaponized it."

"If they did," Tam said, "then maybe it's what they used to kill all these."

"Could be," Bones said, "but we'll have no idea until we find some sort of weapons vault or—"

"Already did."

The three of them turned and found Maddock and Sorensen marching toward them. Following closely behind them were two of the three men Tam had sent away to secure the room. The third was still over near the platform ramp keeping watch.

"Sorensen found a map of the place," Maddock explained, answering an unasked question. "He knew a shortcut to get us past Hoor."

As if triggered by the very mention of the berserker, a shudder vibrated through the floor, followed by a distant—but not too distant—roar.

Bones nodded in Maddock's direction. "I see you've been accessorizing."

Tam followed his gaze and saw the hilt of the enormous weapon on Maddock's back.

"Don't worry," Maddock said, grinning. "I got you one, too."

Sorensen held out an enormous double-sided axe.

"I think you could use this," Sorensen grunted, looking like he'd been through hell.

Smiling as he took it, Bones could hardly contain himself. The axe was made from the same black metal as the doors and the spear.

Realizing this, Tam shot a glance at Maddock. "Where's Gungnir?"

"Safe," Maddock replied simply.

"Where'd you get these?" Bones asked, stepping back to give the axe a few test swings. As he did, its dual-blades ignited with blue energy.

"Bones called it," Tam said, turning to Maddock. "We think they weaponized their power source. It might be able to kill Hoor too."

Maddock glanced to Sorensen who nodded.

"So," Max said, standing behind Maddock, inspecting his new addition, "what's this beast?"

Maddock carefully drew the enormous sword, getting a silent reaction out of everyone when they saw its blade. Its surface roiled like an angry wave but stayed in form. It didn't dance like a serpent did, it just shimmered and twitched like an agitated swell of water. "This is Skofnung, the *Berserker Blade*. It's said to hold the power of a dozen berserkers, infused with their legendary might." He glanced up at Sorensen. "Right?"

The giant gave another quiet nod as the room

shuddered again. The vibrations were stronger now… A lot stronger. And this time, they were accompanied by an agonized scream.

Tam looked back in the direction from which Maddock and Sorensen had come, and flinched as she saw her remaining agent floating a few feet above the ground, suspended in midair, brutally impaled by the wickedly sharp talons of Hoor. Then, suddenly, the man was torn in half, exploding in a mess of gore, and revealing the killer.

"The hell?" Max exclaimed, backing up some.

Hoor was the same twelve-foot height as before but now as thick as a big rig. His arms were still at an extended length as were now his hands, making him look that much more alien. His two large, black, unblinking eyes regarded them, emotionless and yet somehow, full of fury.

What kind of beings could produce such monsters? Tam wondered.

She glanced at the table nearest their position. "Why is he so big and the others barely larger than us?"

"It's his belief and his unbridled rage," Sorensen answered, even as he squared off with Hoor, preparing to meet the charge when it came. "It has completely consumed him. The original inhabitants of this place, while a warring race, were still knowledgeable and advanced—smart. The evidence of that is in everything here. I doubt this place would exist if they all acted as Hoor does now."

Tam took a few steps back. So did everyone else.

"He was insane before becoming a monster," Maddock   added.
The berserker virus only made him more of what he

was."

"I too feel it attempting to take over my body," Sorensen said. He glanced at the people around him. "And my mind."

Bones chimed in. "One part lunacy, add in a double measure of Dr. Banner's own personal creature cocktail, mix thoroughly, and… Hulk smash!"

Hoor didn't press his attack, but instead growled a single word. "Gungnir."

Maddock stepped forward. "Gungnir is gone," he said confidently. "You'll never have it." He raised his sword. "You *can't* have it."

Hoor eyed the large weapon, studying it. Maddock wasn't sure if he/it understood what the blade was or not. Either way, Skofnung was intimidating as hell and even the mighty alien berserker giant seemed to be wary of it.

"Be ready to lay down some suppressive fire if this goes pear-shaped," Maddock said, turning to Tam.

Raising her own Desert Eagle, she nodded and relayed the order to her two remaining agents. Max followed suit but from further behind the others. He was all in, just not quite as all in as the rest of the group.

As Maddock continued to give out orders, Hoor's heavy footfalls quickened and became those of rolling thunder. The floor beneath their feet vibrated and bounced as the monster approached.

Looking left and then right, Maddock got a quick nod from Bones and Sorensen. The three moved as one, charging forward blades at the ready. They'd all fight to the death if necessary.

"Just give me a chance to get inside his reach," Maddock said, planning out his next set of moves. "Let's hope this thing is all it's cracked up to be." He needed to stay ahead of his foe and make sure he could get close enough to deliver the killing blow.

Lord Jesus, Tam thought, *Please let this do the trick.*

SEVENTEEN

Maddock, Bones, and Sorensen all attacked as one. Like ancient warriors of the past, each shouted a battle cry as they charged, hacking and slashing at Hoor's massive frame.

Sorensen was the strongest and therefore opted to fight Hoor one on one for most of the battle. The tactic worked too, allowing the smaller and faster humans to dodge and parry their opponent, but Hoor was not unaware of them. A swipe from the beast opened Maddock's arm. The pain was instantaneous and excruciating. The wound sizzled like acid had been poured into it.

Knocking the clawed hand away, Sorensen swung his axe as hard as he could, connecting with Hoor's flank, causing the creature to wail as it dug in deep. The weapon's energy surged into Hoor's body, inflicting what should've been a deathblow. It didn't kill him, but it did hurt him badly.

Clutching his side, Hoor backed away from the exhausted trio, evidently second-guessing his brutish assault. He had been more careful in the past but the fury that now consumed him had not only given him extraordinary strength, it had also burned away whatever humanity had remained. Including his intelligence.

Hoor, the man who would be a god, was no more. He was just a wild animal.

A twelve-foot tall, nearly invincible wild animal.

Bones hurled his axe at the beast. It rotated in the air a few times before slamming home, directly into Hoor's right shoulder blade, the axe head sinking deep and sizzling with blue fire. With his massive bulk, Hoor couldn't reach the weapon to dislodge it. The wedged blade continued to burn, sending out tendrils of plasma that pulsed down Hoor's arm like veins.

Bones drew his Desert Eagle and, holding it two-handed, unloaded all seven rounds into Hoor, point blank, just like *he* had done to Haugen. Each bullet strike released a coruscation of electric blue energy along with blood that was instantly burnt to black dust.

Yet, Hoor still stood.

Even when Sorensen buried his own axe down in Hoor's chest, he refused to go down.

The beast roared and backhanded Sorensen away, spilling him over the edge of the closest platform. Just like that, their berserker ally was gone, swallowed by the void.

Bones and Maddock regrouped, drawing together, and changing position in order to force Hoor to put his back to the edge of the platform. Right on cue, Tam and her surviving team opened up, concentrating their fire on an impossible to miss target—Hoor's upper torso. Hoor staggered back a step, then another.

Maddock gripped Skofnung tighter while Bones dropped his empty magazine and slammed in a fresh one. As soon as the weapon was ready to go, Maddock charged. Bones expertly aimed and fired, this time aiming for the beast's legs. He needed to keep it off balance long enough for his partner to drive the sword home.

Maddock did exactly that. With one strong upward jab, he drove the black blade into and through Hoor's chest.

Instead of the customary blue energy, a black, smoky version of the stuff poured from the berserker's wounds. An ear-piercing shriek filled the air, but it wasn't Hoor.

The *sword* was screaming….

The souls of the berserker warriors infused to the blade?

Letting go of the still crying weapon, Maddock backpedaled and drew his own gun, unloading as many rounds as he could as quickly as he could. Each trigger pull was like a .50 caliber kick to the head, sending wave after wave of pain and nausea through his already spent psyche.

Falling to one knee in exhaustion, Maddock looked on and watched as Hoor's heavy upper body tilted backward toward the precipice. But before the monster could fall, he caught himself and leaned forward, regaining his balance. He bellowed in pain and anger with every move he made.

But he didn't fall.

Instead, he raised one massive foot, preparing to take a step forward.

Bones was beside himself. "Son of a…"

Like a serpent, a hand snapped out from behind Hoor and latched onto his left ankle, halting his intended retaliation. Grumbling in frustration, the giant struggled a moment, and then vomited a stream of black tar-like fluid. Stumbling, he kicked his caught leg, pulling the hand's owner onto the platform behind him.

"Sorensen!" Maddock shouted, standing in hope.

The still partially-human berserker ripped Bones' axe free from the other creature's shoulder and jumped up and over Hoor's head, yelping in agony as he landed. But without skipping a beat, Sorensen swiped the blade across Hoor's neck, slicing it deep and wide. Blood, along with more of the tar substance, spilled from the wound, and the giant to staggered back.

Enraged and close to death himself, Sorensen threw the blade aside and charged, leading with his talons. At the last instant, Hoor mirrored his attack, so that they impaled each other with their claws when they met.

"No!" Bones shouted.

But it was too late. There was nothing he or anyone else could do to save the man who had become both monster and friend.

With the loudest battle cry yet, Sorensen drove the dying behemoth back toward the yawning drop. Hoor teetered on the precipice for what seemed like an eternity, and then both he and Sorensen were gone, disappearing into the blackness below. Maddock and Bones ran for the platform's ledge, leaning over the side with the hopes of seeing Sorensen.

But he wasn't there. Torbjorn Sorensen was dead, just like he wanted.

"It's done," Maddock whispered.

Bones nodded his agreement and then they both turned…to find Max holding a gun to Tam's temple.

EIGHTEEN

"Don't you do it!" Bones snarled. He took a step forward.

"Stay where you are!" Max gripped her hair, like she was a piece of property and not a human being, driving the barrel of the weapon she'd given him deeper into her skull. Just beyond them, Maddock saw two bodies lying in identical pools of blood. Tam's agents, shot in the back during the firefight.

Bones had no choice but to stop his advance. "What do you want?"

"Isn't it obvious?" Max replied.

"You're here for Gungnir," Maddock said, understanding the motives behind the turncoat's actions. "ScanoGen hired you, didn't they? You were Hoor's transport out of here."

He smiled. "Sorry, gentlemen—and lady." He yanked on Tam's hair again for effect "They paid me a boatload of cash."

"Money!" Tam shouted, cringing as her hair was gripped harder. "You're doing this for money?"

Bones sneered. "Looks like you blew your chance at having dinner with her, Maxie boy."

"Oh, we're having that dinner," he leaned in closer, almost touching her ear. "You see, she's coming with me."

"Not happening," Tam said through gritted teeth. "And if you think that gun scares me, think again."

Max ignored her, kept his eyes on Maddock and Bones.

"You're ex-military, aren't you?" Maddock said,

stalling, looking for an opportunity.

"And let me guess," Bones continued, "you were kicked to the curb for being a little *too* into killing people."

Max shrugged. "My methods weren't exactly smiled upon, so I bailed before they could charge me. They sent someone to keep tabs on me. Once I took care of him, I came here and started over. I couldn't do the merc thing—not with them looking for me, but I knew how to fly, and this seemed like a good place to disappear. Fly tourists by day, move a little 'duty-free' cargo by night. I played nice over the years, offering my services to the local police force, hoping that would keep them off my scent." He gripped Tam's hair harder. "Can't have the Feds mucking up my transport business, can we?"

"But you also got the attention of ScanoGen," Maddock said. "They found out about your past and hired you."

"More like shanghaied me," he replied. "I refused at first, but they threatened to leak my identity to the authorities. Then, after the first payment was made, and I saw the number of *zeros* on its backend, I decided to hell with it, and signed on. Seeing as I'm the only pilot in Vikersund…"

"We hired you on the spot," Tam grumbled, "We were fools."

"Yes, you were."

"Now what?" Bones asked, half-turning in an effort to hide his gun behind his thigh. One shot… But if he missed, he might hit Tam….

"Don't even think about it, Osceola," Max said, sensing his intent. "You may be a good shot, but you aren't that good."

Grinding his teeth, Bones stayed silent and waited.

"Gungnir," Maddock said. "You said you wanted it, right?"

No answer. They knew what he was there for.

"We'll get it for you," he continued, "*if* you let her go."

"Setting terms, are we?" He peeked around Tam's head. "As far as I can see, you aren't in a position to be telling anyone what to do."

"True," Maddock said, "but you don't know where the spear is. Only I do now with Sorensen gone. And I seriously doubt you learned how to read alien inspired runes while in the service. Kill us and you're still without your prize."

"And don't think you can just walk away," Bones added. "Scano doesn't take too kindly to failure. You might not have experience with them, but we sure as hell do."

A sadistic smile spread across Max's face in light of the threat. "Or I could just kill her if you don't show me where it is," he pulled Tam in tight. "Could you live with that?"

Bones knew he couldn't. A glance at Maddock confirmed that he felt the same way. They'd lost too many friends in the past, including men like Haugen and Sorensen—men that were innocent and caught in the middle of something menacing.

But Bones knew Maddock almost always had some kind of backup plan. "I guess we do as he says?"

Maddock nodded.

"Not so fast," Max said. "Leave your guns."

Begrudgingly, they complied, setting the enormous pistols on the floor. Bones looked at Tam who simply nodded for them to go. She knew what could happen if she was left alone but that was a risk they all had to take.

As they headed down the nearby ramp, Bones whispered, "You do have a plan, right?"

Maddock murmured an affirmative. When they were a little further out of earshot, he added. "Besides, I have a feeling Tam may prove to be more of a handful than Max expects."

"Yeah, she's not one to play the damsel in distress," Bones said with a snort of laughter. "That woman is beyond pissed right now. I almost kind of feel bad for the guy. Wait. No I don't."

Max shoved Tam away, sending her stumbling into one of the examination tables, spilling its contents as she did. She muttered a curse under her breath, but not because of the rough handling. Close in, she might have been able to overpower Max, disarm him, but now he had created a buffer between them. If she tried to rush him, he would shoot her before she got two steps.

Shit, she thought, not wanting to do what she was about to. *Ugh… Swear jar.*

She took a quick breath to calm herself—and hide her rage—and then fixed Max with her best come-hither stare. "So, Max, if that's your *real* name, do you honestly find me attractive, or was that all a lie, too?"

Max's eyebrows raised slightly, but he didn't move to her. Seeing that she had his attention, Tam hopped up onto the table, crossing her legs. The heavy winter clothes blunted any sensuality she might have hoped to convey, but it seemed like the right thing to do. She sat and faced him, leaning back in as relaxed a posture as she could muster. For good measure, she threw her shoulders back slightly, sticking her chest out more than normal, getting the desired reaction. Max's eyes glanced down involuntarily, examining her exaggerated curves. Blinking hard, he refocused his attention, meeting her stare. She could see the lust in his eyes.

Gotcha.

"You never answered my question," Tam said, sitting up, uncrossing her legs, then crossing them again, slowly, languorously. She needed to get him closer, preferably so she could kick the gun from his hand. He had stupidly failed to search her. Her Desert Eagle was just inches away in its holster, loaded and ready to go.

He crossed his arms, keeping his pistol in plain sight but *not* pointed at her. "Yes, my name is Max, but it's not Max Nielson. And, yes, I find you *very* attractive."

As he said *very* he stepped toward her.

Just a couple more steps, you asshole... Ugh, stupid swear jar.

"What did you have planned for dinner?" she asked, and then curled her lips in a pout of disappointment. "Or was that all a ruse too?"

She worried that she was overplaying it, being too obvious. Max would see through her charade, and punish her for trying to fool him. But she also knew that once the right buttons were pushed, for some men at least, wishful thinking took over.

But Max remained wary.

"What's this all about?" he asked, pausing his advance.

Tam shyly shrugged, playing coy. "Would you believe it's been a while since anyone has been that open with me?"

As a CIA officer, she had mastered the art of

deception, not to mention using her looks as a distraction.

"You, really? I can't see that."

Tam again pretended to act timid. "Well, in my line of work, you don't often get to that part of a conversation…" She looked around, "but since we have some time to *kill*…"

Accentuating the word *kill* seemed to make Max uncomfortable. He wasn't as in control of himself as she originally thought. It seemed that he was acting against his true nature. While comfortable with killing, it was obvious that Max wasn't used to taking hostages.

Especially one he likes. Tam smiled. *Interesting….*

"What?" Max asked.

Tam realized she'd physically reacted to her thoughts. She swiftly continued their conversation, hoping he wouldn't see through the lie. "Oh, nothing. It's just nice to know when you're liked."

Max took another step forward.

Come on, Maxie, two more.

"It's not hard when that someone looks like you. You're about as easy on the eyes as it gets." He smiled. "I bet your skin is soft, too."

Geez, he's good. Tam thought. *In another lifetime, he'd be a charmer.* "Well, a girl can pamper herself sometimes, can't she?" she retorted.

"I'm sure you can."

Tam smiled again, reeling him in closer.

One more step you bastard.

She leaned forward and bit her lip, a move most men couldn't resist.

Luckily for her, Max was with the majority. He took one long step forward and was met by a combo of kicks.

The toe of Tam's left boot slammed into his groin. Her right foot snapped up high and slammed right into his jaw, sending him reeling backward.

Rolling backward off the table, Tam drew Desert Eagle and fired off two wild shots, hoping it would at least send Max diving for cover. He did, giving Tam the opening she needed. Ducking down, she crawled away from the table, diagonally at first. Then, turned, chaotically zigzagged beneath the high tables, keeping their thick, four-foot-wide base supports between them.

If she could circle around and catch Max by surprise, she might be able to find the guys before they made it to Gungnir.

"You bitch!" Max shouted, spitting red-tinted saliva.

She peeked out from her hiding place and saw him struggling, trying to rise. His body refused to unclench from the bruising blow she'd delivered to his groin, but he was trying to steady himself on one of the tables, using it as a handrail. She couldn't tell if he still had his gun.

Tam considered goading him with another retort, but decided that stealth was a preferable strategy. She scooted quietly as far as the right limit of the platform, then continued along it. She didn't need to surreptitiously check on Max's position; his grumbling and cursing marked his position as effectively as a radar blip. She could tell he was wandering aimlessly.

Guess I bent your compass needle, asshole, she thought, and then winced. This op was really bringing out her worst side. *Probably Bones' influence.*

Moving to the far corner of the room, she ducked under the last of the tables then took a moment to catch her breath and plan her next move. Clutching the massive Desert Eagle in both hands, she got her legs beneath her and readied the weapon.

One shot would do the trick, provided she hit him. A .50 caliber Magnum round could make a man's chest burst like one of Gallagher's watermelons. Even a shot to a non-vital area would probably be fatal, owing to shock trauma and consequent blood loss.

But a miss was a miss, no matter how big the gun was.

Gotta get the shot off first, she thought, not getting too far ahead of herself.

Tam expected Max to have already found his discarded gun and she knew that he not only knew how to use it, but would not hesitate to do so. She would only have a fraction of a second to acquire and fire.

Holding her breath, she listened for any sign of him, but heard nothing. Either he'd stopped moving, or he had recuperated enough to be sneaky.

No help there.

Okay, 3...2...1... Now!

Tam sprang to her feet, quickly getting into a modified Isosceles shooter's stance, her arms forming a triangle with her pistol at the apex, her body and head turning together, searching for her target.

But in the instant that she saw him, something slammed into her middle, bowling her backward.

Max had used the rows of tables like lined-up billiard balls, ramming one into another until they eventually hit her.

As she tried to rise, he bounded over the table tops, and threw himself at her. She barely rolled out of the way in time. He corrected and lashed out with a vicious kick. She threw up a forearm to block it, and felt a flare of pain on contact. The Desert Eagle flew from suddenly nerveless fingers, and slid across the platform, vanishing into the emptiness beyond.

A second swift kick clipped the side of her head, brushing her hair back, but doing little else. Rolling again, she sprang to her feet, turned and faced him.

Max's face was painted in blood—his own—and he was still hunched over, visibly smarting from her attack to his southern regions. He was hurting, and she thought that just might be enough to make up for his superior size and strength in hand-to-hand battle to the death. If it wasn't enough, then at least she'd go down swinging.

Then Max reached behind his back and drew out a long-bladed combat knife.

"Well, crap," she murmured, and for once, didn't even think about the swear jar.

Max advanced, slashing the air between them. Tam retreated a step, looking around frantically for something to use to block his attack. The only thing within reach was the oversized upper arm bone of one of the long-deceased experimental subjects. The rest of the disarticulated skeleton had been scattered to the ground when Max shoved the table.

She snatched it up and held it in front of her, ready to parry any slash that got too close. The bone was called the humerus, if she remembered her anatomy correctly. She could almost hear Bonebrake's making some ridiculous quip about that. The old bone wouldn't be a very effective defensive weapon, to say nothing of having almost no offensive capabilities, and there was nothing "humerus" about that. She needed to get clear of the jumbled tables and make a run for it.

Max darted forward and stabbed at her lower

abdomen. She easily side-stepped, and whacked his wrist with the old humerus. To her amazement, the blow felt solid, the bone a little more substantial than she had expected. Growling, Max drew back, and the slashed up, aiming for her neck. She swatted the blade away, and then jabbed the knobby end of the bone at his face, connecting solidly with his forehead.

As Max staggered back, she flung the bone at him, and then scrambled over the obstacle maze toward the ramp Maddock and Bones had left by.

NINETEEN

Maddock remembered the way to the weapons vault, but what he didn't recall was the blood. It was splattered over every surface of the platforms. Apparently, Sorensen and Hoor fought the entire way down. He tried not to think about it.

"What else do you think is down there?" he asked, trying to make conversation to get his mind off the carnage and the looming threat to Tam.

Bones just shrugged. "No idea, *hombre*, and honestly, I really don't want to find out. What I'd like to do is bring this whole place down and bury it forever." He stopped and looked back the way they came. "Way too much death down here."

Maddock nodded. "Couldn't agree with you more."

Cautiously leaning out over the edge, he peered into the darkness below and thought he saw a faint glow of light. "This place has to have a power source, right?"

"You got me, dude. I'm not sure of anything when it comes to alien tech. For all we know, it could supply its own power because it just can. There may not be a better explanation than that."

Maddock nodded. "You might be right but I think it's worth a look once we sort out our other problem."

"Speaking of that," Bones said, "didn't you say that Sorensen's altered DNA is what allowed him to open the armory? I hate to break it to you but I'm pretty sure we're both human."

"Good point." Maddock knelt next to the closest blood smear and swiped one gloved finger across it, collecting what he hoped would be a viable sample of the altered DNA.

Bones shook his head disparagingly.

"You know, we could circle back and try to get the drop on Max," he said. "If Tam hasn't already taken him out, that is."

"I considered it," Maddock replied, "but I think our chances of saving her and stopping him will be a lot better if we go in loaded for bear. You're not going to believe the stuff that's in here."

He pointed ahead to what he now thought of as "the armory." "This is it."

Bones whistled at the sight. "Okay. I guess you weren't exaggerating."

Maddock led the way to the large container and cautiously touched it with the blood smeared fingertip of his glove. As soon as it made contact with the black exterior, a tremor rippled across the surface, and then it lit up just as before.

"Holy crap.

Maddock went in without delay, heading straight for the collection of spears. He thought he remembered where he left it, but like before, the numbers were so great that it made it tough to tell them apart. "Which one is it?" Bones asked.

"I'm not exactly sure."

"Fan-friggin-tastic," Bones said, rubbing his forehead. "Keep looking. I'm gonna see if I can find something a bit more beastly than what we have."

Maddock nodded and continued his search for the correct spear. The only way to know for sure was to touch them and he decided that would be his last option.

Behind him, Bones was experimenting with one of the axes, activating it and swinging it experimentally.

Blue fire cracked in the air and Maddock smelled the sharp tang of ozone.

Bones set the axe back in its place. "Blades are cool, but Max has a gun. What we need is a ranged weapon. You see anything like that down here?"

Maddock shook his head, more in an attempt to concentrate on the puzzle before him, than in answer to the question.

"Hello gorgeous," Bones said a moment later. Maddock glanced back and saw his friend holding a crossbow and a quiver of bolts, all fabricated from the mysterious black metal. "What do you want to bet these things do a whole lot more than just poke holes in a target."

"Just be careful where you point it," Maddock replied.

At that moment, a shout reached them. "Dane!"

Maddock started involuntarily, even though he immediately recognized the voice.

"Tam?" As Maddock turned toward the entrance, he saw her running toward them.

"I knew you'd kick his ass," Bones chortled.

"Not quite. He's right behind me."

Bones brought the crossbow to his shoulder. "Let him come."

"Don't be stupid," Tam snapped. "He's got a gun. At least find cover."

Bones accepted the rebuke, ducking down behind one of the racks. Maddock and Tam joined him, just as a shot rang out, followed an instant later by the sound of a ricochet. Several more shots followed in quick succession, all of them close enough to confirm that Max had a pretty good idea where they were.

There was a break in the firing and then a shout. "You might as well make this easy on yourself. You can't outrun a bullet."

"No," Bones muttered, "But if he keeps shooting like that, he's going to run out of them."

"He's probably already figured that out," Maddock said. "We need to go on the offensive."

"Is there another exit?" Tam asked, still trying to catch her breath.

"Possibly," Maddock replied, "but I have no idea where it is or where it goes. This is the way Sorensen brought me. He could read the rune glyphs."

A grin spread across Tam's face. She dug into her jacket pocket and pulled out her phone.

"Really?" Bones said. "Is this really the time to post to Snapchat."

"I uploaded a translation program from headquarters just after arriving. It might be able to read the runes for us."

"But these aren't ordinary runes," Bones countered. "This is an alien language."

"If I have to come in there," Max shouted, "I promise your death will be slow and painful. Make it easy on yourself."

Maddock ignored the taunt. "It *could* work. Sorensen said they were close to the Norse runes we all know from history. But right now let's focus on getting around him. If we can get to the upper platform and get between him and the exit, we can end this." He then looked at Tam. "Or pin him down until you can call in some reinforcements."

She shook her head. "I'm not sure that'll work. There's a dead zone up there. It's why our chopper went down. We had a complete instrument failure, including our comms systems."

"Our watches are still working," Bones said. "And your phone."

Tam gave a helpless shrug.

"One thing at a time," Maddock said. "Right now, we need to get out of this container without getting our asses shot off."

"Since you didn't ask for suggestions, I assume you have a plan?"

"Sort of." He scanned the rack of weapons until he found a sword that would serve as a suitable replacement for Skofnung, which Hoor had taken with him into oblivion. After slotting the weapon into the scabbard on his belt, he pointed to Bones' crossbow. "You know where we can get a couple more of those?"

Bones jerked a thumb over his shoulder. "Two rows over."

"All right. We'll fire a spread of bolts. Two apiece in staggered sequence, then run like hell for the exit. Maybe we'll even get lucky and take him out."

"What about Gungnir?" Tam asked. "We'll be leaving the door open for Max to take it?"

Maddock glanced over at the rack of spears. "He'll have to figure out which one it is, first."

"And what if he uses the trial and error approach and turns into a berserker?" Bones countered.

Maddock just shrugged. "Like I said, one thing at a time."

An explosion of blue fire sent Max tumbling. The focal point of the impact was a good twenty feet from where he had been crouching, sparing him the worst effects of the blast energy, but the heat lashed at the exposed skin of his face and neck, scorching the hand that held the pistol so severely that he dropped it. He screamed, in surprise as much as pain, and recoiled away from the dying flash, even as another eruption bloomed to life. The second one was further away, but he still felt the heat on his seared skin. The smell of burnt hair made him gag.

The back of his hand had gone a livid red and was oozing dew-like droplets. He touched this face where he could still feel the heat, and his hand came away wet.

Second-degree burns.

I can buy a new face, he thought, recalling the millions ScanoGen had already delivered to his offshore account. That number would double when he handed over the spear. *But payback is priceless.*

He would kill Broderick and her friends for free.

More explosions followed, some a little too close for comfort, and he'd had no choice but to hunker down and cover up. When a full minute passed without any activity, he raised his head, and then retrieved his gun to begin searching for a target.

He decided not to taunt them this time. Instead, he would sneak up on them, catch them unaware. They were penned up inside the big container—it would be like shooting fish in a barrel.

But as he drew closer, he realized the truth. The explosions had been a distraction to cover their escape. Tam, Maddock and Bones had slipped away while he'd been cowering in terror.

His initial anger passed quickly however when he realized what they had left behind. Standing before the still open armory, he marveled at its contents. He saw axes and swords like the ones Maddock had brought back earlier, and other items too bizarre to describe.

He ventured inside, wandering the aisles in amazement until he found it. The spear… or rather, "Spears," he muttered.

There were dozens of them, lined up side-by-side in multiple racks. And they all looked identical.

"Which one?" he rasped, then shouted, "Which one?"

His sweat stung the freshly scorched skin of his face, but he ignored the pain, willing himself to stay on his feet. In a fit of frustration he thrust out both hands and started grabbing the spears, flinging them aside without even examining them for telltale markings, shouting all the while. "Which one, dammit? Which one?"

Suddenly, one of the black spears grabbed him back. The sensation was as immediate and as vivid as an electrical charge, and it floored him. He howled in pain and then anger as he realized his mistake, but even before he hit the floor, his cries turned into monstrous roars.

He was becoming one of them.

He was becoming a berserker.

TWENTY

They moved quickly up the maze of ramps, and had just reached the lab with its macabre collection of human experimentation, when a familiar roar reached up from the depths.

"Well…." Tam looked like she was about to say something else, something obscene, but then shook her head. "That doesn't sound good."

"One thing at a time," Bones said in a mocking falsetto. "Guess what just became our new 'one thing'?"

"We can stop him," Maddock said, with more confidence than he felt. "Let's get as close to the exit as we can. If we have to, we'll blow the ramps. Trap him down here."

"Is that even possible?" Tam asked. "Those crossbow bolts pack a punch, but this place looks pretty solid."

"We have to try," Maddock replied, "If anyone has a better suggestion, speak up now."

No one did.

They were almost up the first of two ramps when the next roar came. Only, it wasn't muted from the tons of alien metal and stone surrounding them, it was loud and clear, coming from right below their position. Making it to the top, they turned and watched as the beast formerly known as Max stepped into view.

The berserker was built like Sorensen and had the same gray, wolf hair covering most of his body. Max's deformed face was also clear as day, his eyes crimson and full of hate.

And he held Gungnir.

"Well, crap," Bones grumbled, shouldering his

crossbow.

Maddock did the same, and they both loosed bolts simultaneously. The stubby arrows hit home and detonated on impact, blasting the beast off his feet.

But when the smoke cleared, they could see him still gripping the spear, and already rising, shaking off the effects of what should have been a devastating injury.

Then Maddock noticed something else as well. Gungnir was enveloped in what looked like a pulsating corona of black energy, and with each shadow flash, Max seemed to get bigger and stronger.

"Gungnir is giving him a boost," Maddock shouted. "We need to get it away from him."

"I like the concept," Bones said, nocking another bolt. "Just not too clear on the method of execution."

Max roared and stomped his foot, causing the entire platform to shake. Debris began raining down around them, which gave Maddock an idea. "Aim in front of him," he shouted. "And as soon as you fire, turn and run like hell."

Bones did not question the unusual strategy but loosed his bolt into the floor just ahead of Max. For his part, Maddock fired up, into the bottom of the platform above them. The simultaneous explosions rocked the platform, fracturing the floor on which they stood, while dumping tons of rock directly onto Max's head. It wouldn't slow him down for long, but it just might give them time to come up with a more permanent solution.

And like a lightning bolt, inspiration struck.

"Just got a crazy idea." Maddock shouted as they ran.

"I can do crazy," Bones said, reloading on the run.

"We need to head for the longships." He pulled the bloody handkerchief from his pocket. "Maybe they still work."

Bones grin indicated that he approved of that level of crazy, but the moment of elation was short-lived. As they neared the top of the ramp, a massive tremor shook them off their feet. The stone erupted right in front of them, showering them with debris. Maddock blinked the dust away and saw, protruding from the center of a newly created blast crater, a black spear tip, pulsating with shadowy energy. The stone around the crater was cracked and falling away in chunks. Gungnir had accomplished what the crossbow bolts could not—it was bringing down the ramp, and unfortunately Maddock and his friends were on the wrong side of the collapse.

"Run for it!" He shouted.

His warning was unnecessary. Bones and Tam were already moving, heading for the still mostly intact edge of the ramp to their right. Maddock chose the closer, and riskier, route on the left, leaping across the widening fissure. He imagined the ramp crumbling away beneath his feet, and wondered if he would find himself running across the broken pieces as they fell or simply pedaling the air like a character in a cartoon.

But he made it, reaching the next platform where he turned to see how the others were faring. Bones had made it past the crater and was almost to the platform, but Tam was not so lucky.

Just as she passed the crater, the quivering spear tip was yanked back, setting off another tremor that crumbled the ground beneath her, causing her to fall into the crater. Through the gaping hole, Maddock could see the spear, still upthrust, and in the hands of the berserker standing on the ramp below, staring up at Tam, eager to catch her on its point.

As Tam clawed at the edge of the crater, trying to find something to hold onto, Maddock dove for the edge of the pit. He reached out as far as he dared and snagged her coat sleeve, but he knew immediately that he didn't have a good enough hold to pull her back up.

"Bones! A little help!"

Even before he got the words out, Bones was there beside him, using his slightly longer reach to get a better grip on Tam's wrist, which in turn allowed Maddock to improve his hold. Together they pulled, drawing her back to safety, but even as they did, the ramp continued to crumble away beneath them, their combined weight hastening the collapse. Every six inches they gained was lost as the floor beneath Tam fell away, dropping her back into the hole. Below her dangling feet, Max circled and growled like a hungry lion waiting for his prey to fall into his jaws.

But despite the appearance of fighting a losing battle, they were making progress, inching up the slope to find solid ground—relatively speaking—and as soon as they knew it, they hauled Tam to safety with one coordinated mighty heave.

They backpedaled up the slope, dragging her the entire way until they reached the platform where they collapsed as one, falling into one another.

For a second, the three of them just lay there, breathing heavily. Bones began to laugh but stopped as the platform shook again, and the floor beneath him opened as the black point of Gungnir was thrust up through it, missing a much-prized part of his anatomy by mere inches.

They all scrambled back, crab-walking away as the floor around the impact point began crumbling. When they were on relatively solid footing, an extremely pissed-off Bones ran back to the edge of the new fissure and fired his crossbow into it.

There was another explosion and a screech. Bones turned and, as if in response to an unasked question, said, "Because I felt like it!"

Another growl vibrated the air around them, and then, with a loud crunch, a pair of clawed hands appeared at the edge of the newly created hole. Max had jumped at least twenty vertical feet to snag the inner opening of the landing.

"Get to the hangar bay" Maddock shouted, and then shouldered his crossbow and fired.

The bolt detonated right next to Max's thick hand, fragmenting the floor and dropping Max back down, but Maddock knew the berserker would just try again, so instead of reloading and shooting another bolt, he turned and ran after the others, sprinting to the ramp back up to the bay where they had found the longships. Behind them, a series of scrapes and grunts confirmed that Max would soon be joining them.

"If you guys can keep him occupied," Maddock said, "I'll make a run for the hangar bay!"

Bones nodded even as he reloaded. Tam just took aim and let fly, but to everyone's astonishment and dismay, Max knocked the bolt out of the air with Gungnir. The missile did not detonate on contact with the spearpoint, but instead exploded harmlessly against the wall.

"Well… Crap," Maddock muttered, and then turned and ran.

Behind him, Bones and Tam continued their assault without letup, taking turns firing and reloading, but Max swatted the arrows aside, deflecting them as easily as a tennis pro knocking back balls from a machine.

But while he was doing that, his forward movement slowed. He was advancing a step or two for each bolt they fired, but they were backing up the ramp, matching his pace. Unfortunately, their supply of arrows wouldn't last forever.

As he left the battle behind, Maddock knew that, no matter how much damage they did to him, Max would keep coming. It was up to him to find a permanent solution.

If there was one.

TWENTY-ONE

By the time Maddock reached the hangar bay, he was ready to pass out from exhaustion. The air within the facility was cold and hard on his throat and lungs, but he fought through pain and fatigue, knowing that one way or another, it would all be over in just a few more minutes.

He clambered up onto the nearest ship, using a row of precisely cut foot holes in its hull, and rolled over the side and landed hard on the metallic surface. It *gonged* from the impact, rattling his brain. Getting to his feet, he quickly approached the domed section at its center and touched the blood-stained glove fingertip to its surface.

The dome split and began to retract into separate panels, one by one, looking very much like the Sydney Opera House as it did. Not waiting for it to finish, Maddock hopped in and found a single throne-like chair at its core... And nothing else. There was no control console. No instrument panels or display screens.

It felt like the final straw. He'd been counting on being able to figure out how to fly the longship and use what he felt certain would be extraordinary weapons. Defeated, he collapsed into the chair, pounding on the armrests in frustration.

Come on, he thought. *There have to be controls. How do I turn this thing on?*

As if in response, something within the ship hummed to life. He sat up a little straighter, but aside from the sensation of energy pulsing through the vessel, nothing else had changed.

"Voice commands?" he wondered aloud, and then in

an unconscious imitation of Captain Jean-Luc Picard, said, "Computer, lift off."

Nothing.

"Of course not. You don't speak English, do you?" And then he realized his mistake. The ship hadn't reacted to what he'd said, but rather what he had thought.

But how was he supposed to *think* the ship into doing what he needed it to do?

"Guess I'll have to wing it," he muttered. "Ouch. Bad pun. I'll have to learn it on the fly."

Rather than try to give the ship specific commands, he chose instead to imagine that there were controls. He took a deep breath to order his mind, and then visualized a joystick controller, like the cyclic stick on a helicopter. When he had a firm mental image of it, he reached out, closing his finger on the air where he imagined it to be, and pulled back gently.

The hum intensified, and then the deck shuddered beneath him as the craft rose a few inches off the ground.

Marty McFly eat your heart out.

He tilted the imaginary stick to the right, and the ship pivoted in that direction.

Yes!

There was no more time to waste figuring out the nuances. With the ship responding to his nonverbal commands, he swung it around and veered toward the ramp where his friends waited. The ship cruised down the ramp, hovering a foot above the ground like a Star Wars landspeeder.

A moment later, he saw Bones and Tam, their backs to him, and beyond them, the monstrous creature Max had become. Max saw him too. Ignoring the incoming crossbow bolts, he raised Gungnir threateningly in Maddock's direction.

Let's see what this thing can do, Maddock thought. *Weapons systems online.*

A holographic image appeared in front of him like the heads-up display in a fighter jet. It showed a panel on the front of the ship retracting. Then a schematic of the system appeared. It took him a second to realize that he was seeing a scaled-up version of the crossbow arrows. It reminded him of an ancient *ballista.*

Increase speed and prepare to fire.

The longship reverberated beneath him, sending an uncomfortable tingling sensation up his spine, but the craft remained ominously quiet. That was when he realized that the explosions had stopped.

"I'm out!" Bones shouted.

"Me too," Tam answered. "Time to haul ass!"

Tsk. Swear jar, Tamara.

They both turned, intending to flee, and then fell flat as Maddock guided the floating Viking-ship-shaped aircraft between them. He curled his finger around an imaginary trigger, and imagined crosshairs settling dead-center on Max's chest.

Max must have sensed what was coming. Before Maddock could unleash the missile, Max leaped high into the air. Maddock tried to track him, but before he could reacquire the target, Max's arc brought him down squarely on the long ship's foredeck. He hit with the power of a wrecking ball, driving the front end of the ship down onto the ramp with such force that Maddock was almost hurled from the pilot's chair.

He yanked back on the imaginary control stick and the ship responded by jerking backward, bucking the berserker off in the process. Max landed in a heap and rolled down the ramp for a good fifty feet before arresting his slide.

Maddock immediately reversed direction, thinking, *All ahead, full!*

He was thrown back into his seat as if a set of afterburners had kicked in, propelling the ship forward at an incredible rate of speed. It was all Maddock could do to keep his focus on the target—Max. But he didn't fire the weapon.

The ship *was* the weapon.

The craft lurched again until it slammed into Max at full speed, the dagger-like ram at the front piercing clear through the berserker's chest.

The impact threw Maddock forward again, but he was ready for it, bracing himself in place with his feet, and after the initial rebound, he lifted the nose of the craft up, with Max still hanging from the bow.

Maddock knew the injury wouldn't suffice to kill the berserker. Already, Max was recovering from the shock of the wound, gripping the protruding spike with both of his clawed hands, trying to push himself off it.

Both hands… Maddock realized. *He dropped Gungnir!*

Maddock knew he would never have a better chance to end Max's rampage permanently. He calmly curled his finger around a phantom trigger and squeezed.

Fire!

A projectile launched from the concealed weapon's port and immediately detonated.

The explosion tore Max in half, along with the front end of the longship.

The recoil blasted the ship backward, though

incredibly, it remained in the air. Even more unbelievable, Max—his upper half, anyway—was still clinging to what was left of the ship. He stared at Maddock, the fury in his eyes undiminished as he struggled to pull himself closer.

Maddock had one more wild card left to play. If that didn't stop Max, nothing would. Either way, it was going to hurt.

He aimed the damaged ship at the broken platform below, and sent it moving forward. He framed a mental command—*increase velocity to full in five seconds*—and then rose from the chair and hurried aft, leaping from the stern even as the ship continued picking up speed.

Rather than attempting to land on his feet, he fell sideways and rolled, just as he'd been taught to do in airborne jump school. The jolt was no more painful than he'd anticipated, but the slope combined with his leftover momentum, sent him careening down the ramp.

He caught a glimpse of the longship and its remaining passenger disappearing into the emptiness where the laboratory platform had been, and knew that if he didn't arrest his tumble, he would follow it down. Frantic, he drew his sword and drove its tip into one of the ramp's smooth surface.

There was a flash of blue energy on contact, followed by a shower of yellow friction sparks as the sword tip scraped on stone, and then, it caught in a crack.

Please hold! He thought, hanging onto the hilt with one hand. His legs slid over the edge, but then with a jolt that nearly yanked his shoulder from its socket, he stopped. He cried in pain as his full weight hung from the tenuous grip of one hand. Far below, there was a bright flash followed by a thunderous boom and a rising fireball that churned beneath him with all the fury of a berserker, and seemingly, all the heat of an atom bomb.

With his free hand, Maddock tried to pull himself up the rest of the way but couldn't find purchase. Worse, he could feel the blade grinding against the stone, quivering against his weight, slipping….

Then, a strong hand seized his wrist and stopped his plunge. The suddenness of it stabbed through his shoulder join, eliciting a yelp of pain. The sword popped out of the crack, clattered once on the stone and then fell past him into the blazing conflagration below.

Maddock looked up into Bones' grinning face. "It's about freaking time!" he gasped.

"A simple 'thank you' will suffice," Bones said, straining to pull him up without losing his own footing. Tam appeared beside him, grabbing onto Bones' belt. Thus anchored, Bones began hauling Maddock back from the brink. The pain in his shoulder was beyond intense, but he gritted his teeth and endured until he was safely on solid ground again.

"My shoulder," he gasped, "it's out."

Nodding, Bones reached down, braced his foot against Maddock's ribs, and pulled. The joint popped back into place, giving an immediate measure of relief.

Spent, Maddock lay back, happy just to be alive. "Tam," he said, gazing up at the roof of the underground fortress, "next time I ask you for a favor, I want you to remind me what it's really going to cost me."

"I'll try to remember," she replied, laughing.

Bones cautiously peered over the edge. The firestorm was still raging in the depths. "So is that it? Is it over?"

Maddock took in a deep breath and then sat up. "Not while that spear is still around."

He rolled onto his side and used his good arm to push himself up. Seeing his struggle, Bones gave him an assist, gently helping him to his feet. "We have to get rid of it. Permanently."

Together, they made their way back up to the platform. Maddock spotted the spear, right where Max had dropped it. He picked it up, and even though he was wearing gloves, held it cautiously, as he might a pit viper, carrying it back down to the edge overlooking the abyss. As he made his way down, he thought about the undiscovered secrets that lay below—the answers to the question of who built the fortress and why, and the mysterious power source that made it all possible. Hoor and Sorensen were down there, too. Almost certainly dead, but maybe not.

"Tam," he said as he gazed down into the flames. "You need to destroy this place. Blow it to hell. Collapse the cavern and bury whatever's down there forever."

He expected an argument, expected her to cite national security concerns as a reason to conduct further investigations, but she surprised him by nodding. "I don't think anyone's ready for this stuff," she said.

Satisfied, Maddock held Gungnir out in front of him and let it fall into the inferno. "There. Now it's over."

TWENTY-TWO

A week later
Outside Vikersund, Norway

Tam Broderick kept her promise to Maddock both literally and figuratively. After they made their escape from the alien complex—Maddock sealing the mystery metal with a touch from his bloodstained glove, which he then burned to ensure that the door would never again be opened—and trekked back through the tomb entrance, she immediately began spinning an intricate web of deception and obfuscation to explain everything that had happened.

All of those who had been lost—Sorensen and Haugen, and all the members of the ScanoGen strike team—would forever be relegated to the ambiguous status of "missing, presumed dead." Officially, Max and the rest of Tam's team had perished in a helicopter accident, of which she was the only survivor.

The report she eventually filed with her superiors told the truth up to a point. She downplayed the physical effects of the berserker transformation, making it sound more like a variant of the rabies virus. She truthfully reported that the spear had been incinerated, but did not mention the alien fortress or its trove of energy weapons. Her superiors signed off on the report and agreed with her recommendation to sanitize the area, which was why, just eight days after emerging from the secret tomb of King Harald Fairhair, she was back.

She placed the last of the explosive charges, inserting the blasting cap. The charge was one of several placed at strategic points around the tomb, all of them daisy-chained together so that, when she activated the detonator from a safe distance, they would blow simultaneously, dropping the tomb and everything above it into the cavity below, permanently burying the alien fortress. She connected the blasting caps to the end of a spool of speaker wire, but she did not immediately leave the tomb.

She had promised Maddock that she wouldn't reveal what they found to anyone, but that didn't mean she wasn't going to satisfy her own curiosity about the place before closing the door on it forever.

She set the spool on the ground near the exit, and then retrieved her rucksack and headed back into the maze of corridors. When she came to a solid wall of the black metal, she doffed her pack and took out a sealed plastic package, which contained what looked like a latex thumb cot. She opened the package and unrolled the cot on to her index finger. It fit snugly and glistened with a clear viscous fluid. The fluid was mostly silicone gel but mixed into it was a bit of berserker blood plasma from a sample she had surreptitiously taken during the earlier visit. She touched it to the metal surface, and opened the door to the lower levels.

Everything was as they left it—the bodies and the blood, though the latter had dried to a black crust.

The ruined platform was completely impassable, but Tam had come prepared. She unlimbered her pack a second time, and took out climbing equipment—a rope, harness, and a rappelling device. She had also brought along an Atlas powered auto-ascender. She wouldn't need it for the climb down, only when it was time to head back up.

Once her anchors were set, she stepped off the platform, abseiling down into the depths. The fire had long since burned itself out, and while there was a faint glow emanating from the darkness, it wasn't bright enough to see by. Always prepared, she had brought along night-vision goggles.

The facility was much larger than any of them had originally thought, taking up a sizeable portion of the mountain's interior. She couldn't fathom how such an architectural marvel had been constructed, and wondered how long it had taken to complete.

Decades at a minimum. Maybe even centuries.

It probably would've been a mere blink of the eye for the aliens.

As she neared the end of her rappelling rope, the ground came into view below her. She now realized that there were dozens of passages branching off from the central section, with more ramps and landings. She could spend a lifetime exploring them all, but unfortunately, all she had was a few hours.

"Unbelievable," she said to herself, although keenly aware of the millions of tons of earth above and around her.

Off to her right lay the charred and broken bodies of Hoor and Sorensen. Their remains had been pulverized by the fall and scorched by the firestorm, but she recognized the shattered remains of the alien weapons they had used in their battle. She was heartbroken but also relieved. She had secretly harbored a suspicion that the berserkers might have survived even that catastrophic event, and worried that Hoor would eventually claw his way out of the mountain in order to resume his reign of terror.

Definitely dead.

"Thank God I'm alone…"

She let her last comment hang in the air. She hoped that was true. She still had to account for Max. She had brought her pistol along, but if Max had survived everything else, it was unlikely that her little pop gun would do much more than tickle his fancy.

As she peered into the darkness, looking for the wreckage of the longship, she saw a small blinking white light twenty yards ahead, flaring brightly in the display of her night-vision goggles.

"What the…" She flipped the goggles up and decided to investigate the old-fashioned way. Clicking on her flashlight, she approached the light, which now appeared to be red.

"Well, Maddock, you were right. I think it's safe to say we have power."

The light shone from a large and otherwise featureless console—about the size of an ordinary desk— made entirely of the black metal.

Impulsively, she slipped on the finger cot and touched the red light. It instantly flicked to blue and then, so did everything all around her. She winced as the brightness stung her eyes.

"And there was light," she murmured, quoting Genesis. "And it was good."

The illumination revealed far more than she had imagined possible. Although the area around her was a ruin—destroyed by the exploding longship and debris from the collapsed platforms above, further out she could see orderly rows of containers, each about twelve feet long by six feet wide by four tall, and spaced about ten feet apart. They stretched as far as her eyes could see.

Something about the containers was eerily familiar. They looked like Egyptian sarcophagi.

Her hands trembling, Tam moved toward them, stopping to examine the first one she came to.

The containers were made of the black metal, but the top panel was transparent, revealing the contents. Tam was not at all surprised to see the outline of a body inside, still and unmoving, floating in a viscous green fluid, looking very deep space SyFy channel.

The fluid obscured the figure within, revealing only an outline, but it was an enormous monstrous outline. Inhuman.

A berserker.

But why…?

The answer hit her like a slap.

"They're stasis pods," she said, her words catching in her throat. "Good Lord, they're alive…"

She, and everyone else, had just assumed that the bodies in the lab were failed experiments when trying to build the berserker army. They'd been wrong. Fairhair had built his army, and it was here, alive and waiting for a general to lead them.

Fairhair was long dead, but the means to control the berserkers had survived through the ages.

If Hoor had succeeded in bringing Gungnir to the lowest levels, nothing would have prevented him from waking and unleashing the unstoppable army against humanity. She turned away, horrified by what she had just beheld, and even more so by how close they had come to disaster.

That was when she saw it.

In the burned and blasted crater, surrounded by shapeless pieces of debris, Odin's spear—Gungnir—

waited. It had not been destroyed by either fire or fall—nothing on earth could destroy it, she now realized—but had pierced the stone floor, and now protruded vertically like the fabled sword in the stone of Arthurian lore.

She did not, even for a moment, consider trying to retrieve it. Maddock was right. Possessing a weapon like Gungnir—a weapon no one on earth could ever hope to comprehend—would only end in disaster. She had to bury it, seal it deep underground and hope that no one ever learned of it.

Giving the spear a wide berth, she hurried back to the ropes. After threaded the line into the Atlas auto-ascender and clipping it to her climbing harness., she squeezed the trigger control and was whisked off the ground.

The ascent seemed to take forever, and when it was done, she left the ropes and gear behind, all but running back through the tunnels to reach the tomb. She used the finger cot with its alien DNA to close the black metal vault door, and when that was done, she peeled the latex away and tossed it into the open coffin of King Harald. Then, she connected the wire from the spool to the demolition charges, and hastily exited the tunnel, unreeling the wire as she went. The spool held five hundred feet of wire; she covered that distance in less than two minutes, exiting the cavern and continuing down the stone path as fast as her legs would take her. When she got to the end of the reel, she connected the detonator to it, and with trembling fingers, squeezed the trigger, sending a small electrical charge through the wire to the blasting caps in the charges.

There was no visible blast. Just a tremor that resonated through the ground, shaking snow from the trees.

Tam let out the breath she had been holding for what seemed like forever.

"Now it's over," she murmured, remembering Maddock's declaration.

But she knew, deep down, that it would never truly be over. She had not destroyed Gungnir or the army it could command, and someday, maybe in a hundred years or even a thousand, someone would learn what lay hidden deep underground, and in their arrogance, they would try to control that terrible power. When they did, the berserker army would rise.

And mankind would fall.

EPILOGUE

The hallway was empty, the building dead silent. Sam Grieco caught himself holding his breath as he moved slowly toward his destination. This was a meeting he was not looking forward to.

He rounded the corner and almost collided with Corrie Kovack, the tall, leggy blonde he'd been dying to ask out since she'd joined the staff six months ago. He'd approached her half a dozen times, but never quite mustered the courage.

"Oops. Sorry!" she said, flashing a wide smile. Her straight, white teeth and blue-green eyes sparkled.

"My fault," Sam said, taking in an involuntary step backward. "Got my mind on other things."

"A meeting with the Revenant will do that to you." Her smile vanished as she flicked a glance back over her shoulder.

"The Revenant? Is that what we're calling him now?"

"Not to his face," Corrie whispered. Her expression grew serious. "What do you think happened to him?" she whispered.

"Looks to me like he got his throat slashed, but whoever did it didn't press down hard enough. That and he's obviously been burned."

"I know, but all the reports said he was dead. And then he just shows up. No explanation."

Sam shrugged. "Who knows? Probably discovered some new, crazy-ass pharmacological down in the jungle."

Corrie looked back in the direction of the office door, then moved in close. Sam shivered. He could smell her perfume, feel her breath on his ear as she whispered.

"I heard he's been dabbling in the occult. Something about a witch from some Central American cult."

Sam doubted the man had been brought back by magic, but he wasn't going to argue. This was the longest conversation he'd ever had with Corrie, and he wanted to keep it going.

"Nothing he does would shock me."

"I know." Corrie nodded. "I shouldn't even be talking about this. But I can trust you, can't I." She winked, sending another shiver down his spine.

Sam wanted to come up with some witty reply, but all he could manage was, "Yes."

"Good." Corrie reached out and gave his arm a squeeze. "You're one of the good ones in here."

"That's what she said," he blurted, and immediately felt his cheeks burn. That was the best he could do?

To his surprise, she let out a genuine laugh. "That's my favorite show."

"Mine, too." Before he could stop himself, he blurted, "Want to come to my place tonight? Order some takeout and binge-watch season three?"

"That's the best season. Just email me your address and what time to be there."

"Really? I mean, great!"

"See you tonight." She flashed another dazzling smile and moved gracefully away.

Buoyed by his success, Sam virtually bounced the remaining steps to the office door. He rapped twice and waited.

"Come," the voice on the other side barked.

As Sam stepped into the office, his joy began to dissipate. The old saying about "killing the messenger" echoed in his mind.

Don't kill me. Not when I finally got a date with Corrie.

Sam hesitated, stared at the man on the other side of the desk. The figure stood with his back to the door, silhouetted in the afternoon light that streamed in through the picture window behind the desk. Silence hung between them, Sam's heart drumming. Finally, he cleared his throat.

"Sir, I have a report from Norway."

The man let out a long, tired sigh. "I can tell by your tone of voice that the news is not good." Alex Scano turned around slowly, rested his hands on his desk, and stared a hole through Sam. His brown hair had been cropped short. Red patches on his face and hands where he had been burned shone angrily in the bright light. A livid red scar traced a path across his throat.

How did you survive? Sam wondered.

"Sir, the mission failed." He hastily sketched out the details, eager to leave before Scano lost his temper.

To his surprise, Scano remained calm.

"Maddock and Bonebrake, you say?"

"Yes, sir."

Scano nodded slowly. "Very well."

Sam was dumbfounded. He had expected Scano to rage, to fire him, even order him killed. But his demeanor was downright placid.

"You're surprised," Scano observed. 'It's all right. I know I have a reputation for being temperamental."

Sam thought it best not to agree with the assessment, but to merely hold his tongue.

"I have plans already in motion to deal with Maddock and Bonebrake. This bump in the road will only make it all the more satisfying when they come to fruition."

Sam nodded. "Is there anything else you need from me, Sir?"

"Not today. Why don't you knock off early? I imagine you'll want your place spic and span when Corrie comes over."

Sam forced a smile to cover his sheer terror. How much had Scano heard? As the thought flitted through his mind, Scano reached inside his jacket.

Oh, God. He's going to shoot me.

Rooted to the spot, Sam watched as Scano took out his wallet, withdrew three twenty-dollar bills, and slid them across the desk. "Dinner is on me. I like you and Corey. You're dependable."

"Thank you, sir." Forcing his hand not to tremble, he picked up the bills and stuck them in his pocket. "We both enjoy working here."

"Call me Alex. We'll be working more closely together starting tomorrow. Have a good night."

Sam knew he'd been dismissed. Relief flooding through him, he turned and headed for the door. He was almost out of the office when Scano spoke again.

"Sam? One more thing."

Sam's throat clenched, and an icy chill ran through him. The money, the compliments, had it been a mind game? He turned back toward Scano, now certain he would see a gun in his boss's hand. Instead, Scano was smiling.

"Tell Corrie that I like the name Revenant. I might even keep it."

The End

ABOUT THE AUTHORS

David Wood is the USA Today bestselling author of the action-adventure series, The Dane Maddock Adventures, and many other works. He also writes fantasy under his David Debord pen name. When not writing, he hosts the Wood on Words podcast. David and his family live in Santa Fe, New Mexico. Visit him online at davidwoodweb.com.

Matthew James is the critically acclaimed author of eight titles, including *Blood & Sand*, *Mayan Darkness*, *Babel Found*, *Elixir of Life*, *Plague*, *Evolve*, *Dead Moon*, and now, *Berserk*. He lives in West Palm Beach, Florida with his family. You can visit him at:
www.Facebook.com/MatthewJamesAuthor
www.JamestownBooks.Wordpress.com
Instagram: MatthewJames_Author
Twitter: @MJames_Books

82392251R00120

Made in the USA
Middletown, DE
02 August 2018